Autographs

ALSO BY BRENDA COOPER

Fremont's Children
The Silver Ship and the Sea
Reading the Wind
Wings of Creation
The Making War (forthcoming)

Project Earth
Wilders
Keepers

Ruby's Song
The Creative Fire
The Diamond Deep

The Glittering Edge
Edge of Dark
Spear of Light

Standalone Novels
POST
Mayan December
Building Harlequin's Moon (with Larry Niven)

Collected Short Works
Cracking the Sky
Beyond the Waterfall Door

BOOKS BY DANIELLE ACKLEY-McPHAIL
Yesterday's Dreams
The Die is Cast
(with Mike McPhail)
A Legacy of Stars

BOOKS BY JOHN A. PITTS
Forged in Fire
Black Blade Blues
Honeyed Words
Night Terrors

STORIES OF FREMONT'S CHILDREN

EDITED BY **BRENDA COOPER** AND
DANIELLE ACKLEY-McPHAIL

eSpec Books

Pennsville, NJ

PUBLISHED BY
eSpec Books LLC
Danielle McPhail, Publisher
PO Box 242,
Pennsville, New Jersey 08070
www.especbooks.com

ISBN: 978-1-949691-05-4
ISBN (ebook): 978-1-949691-04-7

Cover Design: Mike McPhail, McP Digital Graphics
Interior Design: Danielle McPhail
Double DNA Vector Icon © vikivector, www.stock.adobe.com
Cover Art: The Healing Power of Nature © psychoshadow, www.stock.adobe.com
Silver Ship Art: © Mike McPhail, McP Digital Graphics

Dedication

To Friendship.

This series is about friendship and family,
and it took both friendship and family
to birth this book of stories.

Thank you.

CONTENTS

INTRODUCTION

These stories, fragments, and poems are set in the Fremont's Children universe. This is the first world that I created, and the setting for my first three solo science fiction novels as well as all of the stories and poems in this book. It's enjoying a renewal. The original series was always meant to be four books, but only three came out since the great recession ate book two in the series. But that's a story for another time, and maybe I'll tell it when the last book comes out. The books have been releasing in beautiful 10th Anniversary editions, and this set of stories is designed to complement the books. But if you've come to this on its own, don't worry; the words here will stand alone fine.

The Silver Ship and the Sea was drafted during the run-up to the Iraq war. It's meant to show the costs of war. It's also about belonging and family. Reading the Wind is about the people we may become, people who can change their looks and strength and abilities, and who can create life. *Wings of Creation* continues that theme, looking more closely at how the creations of others might be taken advantage of. *The Making War* is about finding a moral peace when you have too damned much power. Throughout these books, the heart of the story is about six people who are rejected as children for being different, and yet who find a way to grow up and change the course of history for five worlds.

These poems, stories, and fragments of data are pulled from the time before *The Silver ship and the Sea* begins through the end of the timeline in *Wings of Creation*. They are set on three different planets.

I'm not much for overly long introductions. After all, in the end, fiction either works for you or it doesn't. I hope you enjoy these words.

Brenda Cooper

Prolog: The Silver Ship and the Sea

Brenda Cooper

From the story of Chelo Lee,
dated July 17, year 222, Fremont Standard,
as brought to the Academy of New World Historians

Fremont was discovered in the year zero. Zero always begins the marking of a new planet's time, as if it did not exist before humans found it.

My story did not begin until after year zero, but I should tell you about discovery. About zero. Zero is full of infinite possibilities. Five bright metallic probes swooped in from Inhabited Space, circled a wild planet, and then, one by one, plunged to the surface. Three landed in oceans, reporting salt and brine and signs of life. One disappeared entirely, possibly swallowed by the molten Fire River that issues from the mouth of the volcano Blaze, the hot soul of the continent Islandia. The fifth probe landed in Green Valley, where we live today. It reported that humans could breathe the air and that carbon-based life existed abundantly on Fremont.

And so, a hundred years later, the thousand colonists came. They fled Deerfly, a planet much like Fremont, much like Earth. Deerfly took its name from the shape of one of its seas, like a deer with wings. The shape is painted on the outside of the thousand colonists' ship, *Traveler*.

They parked *Traveler* in orbit, taking seven small planet-hoppers to the surface, shuttling up and down for months with people and supplies. Being careful. Even so, Fremont's predators began killing them even before they all made it to the surface.

For Fremont was joyous, riotous, very alive, and very wild. The probes mapped a moment in time: a snapshot, not a movie. If more had found our valleys, had found the two livable continents (Islandia and Jini), had found the wide grass plains, the colonists might have been better prepared.

Fremont rumbles and moves and shifts. Its blood flows across the surface in red-orange rivers and slides into its waters, sending steam hissing and spewing to honor the marriage of water and fire. Fremont's grasses and plants and animals are sharp-edged and sharp-toothed. Edible, but only once their defenses are breached.

New colonies often fail. Fremont's almost did.

After a full hundred years, Fremont hosted only fifteen hundred people, now third and fourth and fifth generation, ragged and hungry and tired. Two hundred wanderers, called roamers, traveled the continent of Jini. Twice a year, they returned to Fremont's one city, Artistos, nestled between the Lace Forest and the Grass Plains. The roamers planted and tended a continental network of information feeds, which they used to document the beauty and danger of Fremont. They fought to gain the knowledge and experience needed for the colony to survive. Everyone else lived in Artistos, behind fences.

Artistos's planners designed for five thousand. Planners laid streets out and builders put up the first houses. Guild halls ringed the town's center, Commons Park. People tended the park, filled granaries, and gathered to learn and share stories, fears, and songs.

The colonists' stubborn clutch on the values that drove their flight from Deerfly made Fremont even harder. They claimed true humanity, refused to be augmented, to improve their physical nature to better match the wild things that surrounded them.

Two surprises landed on the Grass Plains in the year 200, ships bearing my parents and others like them. *New Making* and *Journey* were nimble enough to land on the empty concrete pads, Artistos's spaceport, searing the ground around them black and bending the yellow-green whip grass flat. They bore a mere three hundred people, but three hundred altered. Modified for intelligence, for strength, for quickness, for long life. My early education on Fremont taught me they were evil, but they were my own people.

We now call what happened the Altered War, or the Ten Years War, and hope that no one else comes to make another one. Most say it started over scarce food supplies, or over demands from the altered that the original humans follow their footsteps. Others whisper that it started over bad advice given intentionally to the newcomers.

I don't care. I do not know why it became war. Why couldn't we all live here? After all, we believe both Jini and Islandia are habitable, even though no human lives on Islandia yet. But never mind, for that fact matters later, but not now.

However it began, in the end fewer than a hundred altered survived. They fled Fremont, taking the *Journey*. Half of the first colonists died. One altered had been left behind: Jenna—blind in one eye, one arm lost, but fast as a paw-cat. Jenna ran, climbed, hunted, and outfoxed everyone who tried to kill her.

And us. The only altered, as far as we know, born on Fremont.

There are six of us; children of the dead. We were adopted, mostly separated. Alicia and Liam, both three years old, went to two groups of roamers, while four of us stayed in town. My brother and I remained together, adopted by Artistos's leaders, Therese and Steven, as a sign of the end of the war. Kayleen went to the popular, and barren, biologist, Paloma. Bryan became part of a large houschold in the builder's guild. I was five at the time and Joseph two. Kayleen and Bryan were both four. So I was the oldest, the one who had to keep us alive.

My new mother, Therese, once told me the altered designed our unique talents for Fremont. The words she used were, "They made you for this place." My first parents must have been made for Fremont as well, but made for the snapshot the probe sent back, not for the real place.

We did not grow up in time to do whatever they made us for.

They are, of course, gone, or dead. Their ship, the *New Making*, stands upright where it landed. The ground surrounding the ship is still mostly bare and black in a circle as wide as the ship is tall. Wider than twenty of us lying down. It reminds us of our heritage. It remains locked, inaccessible.

The Altered War ended twelve years ago. The first colonists returned to an enemy that had harried their flank, and in some ways had become their ally, as they fought the altered. They returned to the struggle to survive Fremont.

I barely remember my first parents. They floated in and out of our lives like smoke, coming to our tents late at night, exhausted, then leaving again at daybreak. I do remember Chiaro, one of the last altered to be killed. She raised us, and she was our teacher. To this day, although the pain has shrunk to a small stone in my belly, I miss Chiaro. Therese told me once that Chiaro saved us, bartered her own life for the six of us, claiming that we would someday be helpful.

Therese and Steven treat me well enough, and I respect them. At first, they were our captors more than our parents. It was only when we became old enough to work alongside them, old enough to begin learning our abilities, how to offer them carefully and subtly, that they began to treat us with respect and, perhaps, as family. My brother Joseph loves them, I think. He has no memory of our first parents. He has little memory of the first few years we lived in Artistos. He does not recall being watched carefully, as if he would turn and bite the hands that brought him breakfast. He does not remember the time before Artistos began to appreciate our abilities, to begrudgingly allow us to participate in the life of the colony.

And why not appreciate us?

I am very strong, and think well about spatial relationships, about trajectories, about trends, about interactions between people. Those skills let me become quietly important, useful without being easily noticed. Joseph, like me, has no external physical enhancements, although he, too, is strong and fast with keen senses.

His extraordinary gift is built deep inside him. He absorbs and synthesizes and directs data, balancing multiple streams in his brain, accepting many inputs, seeing multiple current moments, and correlating information. He is so earnest in his desire to please that most love him. Again, I ask why not?

We all need each other to survive.

How the Roamers Got
Their Wagons

Brenda Cooper

Joy Linda threw a stick onto the fire, and the yellow-gold flames flashed toward the night sky, making her lean away from their sharp heat.

Bart sat near her, the fire throwing shadows and light on his grizzled face. "Are you cold?"

Her back felt cold and exposed but she didn't say so. "Fire keeps the forest away."

He laughed. "For now."

His laugh ran up her spine, sharp and painful. She ignored him. Old boor. Just outside the circle of light, she felt the soft footfalls of predators walking a circle around the camp. Leaves rustled. A low growl dug even deeper under her skin than Bart's laugh.

She tossed a heavier piece of wood on the flames, and then another, another, another. The safety of the light washed over her in waves.

An hour passed, two.

The pile of firewood grew smaller.

"Go to bed," Bart told her.

She grimaced at the command. "Later."

He was a big man, round and slightly stooped, sixty or so years old. He was a true colonist, born on the spaceship that brought them all here. She had been born on the ship, but all of her memories were here. Maybe it was the age difference that made him so imperious. Maybe he was just imperious. In spite of his command, she picked up a stick.

He plucked it from her hand before she could fling it on the fire. "Stop worrying. We have our stunners."

Which was not enough. She glared at him. They should be a bigger group. But he'd wanted to get back for a meeting of some kind, and he always talked about how he wasn't afraid.

Well, she was. But she didn't let that turn her gaze from him.

He stared back, his dark eyes wreathed in wrinkles and yet still full of power. He was waiting for her to give up. He'd done that ever since she was his student at the Guild Hall, and even though she could resist his unrelenting gaze more easily than she had then, she did eventually look away.

She climbed into her tent and zipped it shut. She lay curled under her one blanket, facing Fremont's forest, her stunner clutched close to her breast.

A death scream split the night, the sound somewhere between far away and a medium distance away. A round of barking snarls from a pack of demon dogs announced the killers, the sound bouncing between ridges.

Something small rustled outside near her feet.

Bart shifted his weight, one foot scraping against the ground.

A night bird chittered from a tree just outside the camp's clearing, then fell silent.

Her own breathing sounded loud and too fast.

A pebble bounced off her tent. She sat straight up, loosened the safety on her stunner.

"Don't come out," Bart whispered.

Terror blew her awake. She slid to a crouch, holding her weapon, focusing on keeping her hands still.

Silent seconds followed, slow seconds full of peril.

She wanted to stand, to see outside. To help. But in the dark of a Fremont night, it was best to be still.

Surely the coals were still hot. Bart should throw more wood onto them.

No sound offered any clue, although the continued silence promised danger.

Weight slammed against the side of her tent, a sharp blow. Something huge and full of muscle knocked her down. Fabric tangled around her, trapped an arm, ripped her stunner from her fingers and folded her inside.

A strangled cry knifed the silence, then a crunch of bone.

The cry had been human. Bart.

The tent still trapped her and she stayed as still as possible, as quiet. She forced herself to breathe through her nose.

Leaves snapped. Something growled, low and intense. A growl of effort laced with menace. The predator had been silent until it struck.

Not demon dogs. Rhu had named them for their noise.

A cat. Paw-cat, probably. But there were others. Paw-cats were bigger than humans. If they stood on their hind legs, they were taller. Silent predators, and strong. More than one, usually.

She'd never seen one, but two people had died by their claws. Most of the wildlife on Fremont didn't eat humans, but it was happy enough to kill them from time to time.

She breathed shallowly, slowly. *Please don't find me. Please don't hear me.*

Something scraped across the ground. The cat, dragging Bart's body. She'd heard his neck snap. That had to have been what she heard. She was sure of it.

Moving, breathing loud, *existing.* All of those things could kill her.

The cat's claws scraped across rock, the sound setting her bones thrumming with fear. Again. And then it was a few feet past her, bushes rustling.

Bart. She hadn't liked him, but she hadn't wished him harm. Her father had died out here, and a few years later, her first crush, a boy named Jimmie.

It could be her. It could be her right now. Any moment. She bit down on her thumb to still her fear and listened until the cat could no longer be heard. She kept listening, kept still, kept her attention on every sound in her body and in the forest around her until light began to stain the sky with safety.

She left everything behind. Notebooks. Broken tent. Specimens. They were all dead things anyway, rocks and plants and the skull of something large with long teeth. At least she didn't have to preserve some living rodent or plant they were bringing back.

She left her own pack, although she had the presence of mind to grab her water.

The sun beat down on her back as she wound down the High Road on foot, alone and fast. The road was flat and wide, one of three roads carved carefully by machine in the first ten years of the colonization. The humans had made the roads, but the wild things of Fremont used them as well, and here and there she saw the small rounded hoofprints of djuri or the clawed prints of four-footed predators.

They hadn't even named all the predators yet.

Even though she left at dawn, it took almost until midday to get close enough to look down on Artistos, spread across the top of a cliff above the wide, grassy plains. She felt eyes on her the entire trip. Fremont, watching and waiting, hoping she'd show weakness. Real or imagined, the sense of being watched kept her walking fast and likewise kept her from breaking into a run. If she had learned anything from this planet, it was never to show her fear.

As soon as she felt the slight frisson of passage through the boundary and the bells rang friendly entry, she collapsed on a rock and breathed and breathed and breathed.

Artistos was the only town on Fremont. It had been carefully planned for far more people than actually lived in it, and the outskirts were empty. She passed unused roads and cleared sites waiting for buildings. Joy crossed three empty "streets" before she spotted her mother and the chief scientist, Deborah. They waved as soon as they saw her.

She broke into a run.

Her mother's arms smelled of flour and salt, her cheeks of oil, and the tears she spilled down her face left tracks in the flour dust that whitened her skin. Her mother murmured in Joy's hair. "We expected you yesterday."

Deborah asked, "Where's Bart? He's not supposed to leave you, not even inside the bells."

Joy shook her head, unable to force the words she should say though her teeth.

Deborah pressed. "He's dead, isn't he? Stupid lunk of a man up and died on you."

Joy spit out a word. "Cat."

Deborah's eyes widened. She looked like she expected Joy to say something else, but she had no more no words right now, nothing she wanted to say to anyone. But it was a long time before she let her mother go. They walked back to town in silence. Joy felt utterly drained. Her mother was almost always quiet, and Deborah had a furious frown on her face and looked like her jaw was clamped shut.

All of the scientists had small rooms in town. As the newest member of the science team, Joy's was one of the smallest. It felt safe. She stayed there all the next day except for meals. Then again the next. The walls felt like heaven.

After three days, the knock she had been expecting came. She called out, "It's unlocked!"

Deborah came in and sat beside her, pulling her bedcovers covers away from her shoulders. "You have to come out. The colony needs you."

"When is the funeral?"

"Tonight. You must come." Her lips thinned and her jaw tightened. Deborah's version of Bart's stare. "And then you must rejoin us. Come back out. We'll make sure you're part of a bigger group."

Joy struggled up and sat, staring out of the window at the hostile planet that surrounded them. "There are people who don't have to leave. Including my mother."

"And there are more people who do. We are the only force—"

"—who can keep the city safe," Joy finished. She looked at Deborah, hesitated, and then blurted, "I heard him die. *I could have died.* I need something simple for a few weeks. Like laundry. Or cleaning the barn."

"You're too able-bodied for those chores." Deborah brushed her graying hair from her face. "We cannot let you become like your mother. There aren't enough people to waste one so young. Your mother agrees."

Joy could imagine how that conversation went. Her mother had often asked her to stay behind, so Deborah must have given her no choice. Deborah seldom allowed choices.

Deborah continued, "Your mother could not come to tell you this. She couldn't bear it."

They had let her mother withdraw when her father was killed. "I know."

"We need you."

Joy let out a long breath. "I'm afraid."

"Of course you are. We are all afraid." Deborah's gaze was steady and long, and utterly uncompromising. "I flew here with Bart. We built a wall together, and designed the Science Guild rules together. I will mourn him tonight." She put a hand on Joy's knee. "I know he wasn't your favorite teacher, but he was a good man."

Joy shifted her leg so Deborah's hand slid away. "I know my duty to the dead."

"And the living. You must return to your work tomorrow."

What would happen if she refused? Would the old woman force her? Would they put her outside the boundary and let the demon dogs or the yellow snakes or the paw-cats eat her?

Probably not. But she couldn't imagine crossing the boundary. Even the thought of it made her stomach twist and jump. "I'll do something useful tomorrow."

The look on Deborah's face blended anger and sorrow. Joy didn't see the point of either. They should be afraid.

After Deborah left, Joy paced. After ten minutes, she knew that Deborah was right. Not about the anger. But she did need to do *something* for the colony. Artistos could not afford dead weight. After enough pacing, she finally had an idea.

She went to the Science Guild Hall. All five students were just leaving for labs after morning lessons, and so there were computers available. She found the librarian, Johannes, and asked, "Can I have an extra notebook? I left mine behind when Bart was killed."

Johannes looked pained, and Joy suspected he minded giving her the notebook. But she took it and began executing careful searches and taking detailed notes. Johannes walked by three times, peering at what she drew. The fourth time, she held up her hand to stop him. "Go ahead. Ask."

"Is that a wagon?"

"Yes."

"Good idea." He sat down at the computer beside her and brought up other images for her to look at. "It has to be smaller," she said.

"But big enough to carry specimens. You could go further."

She shivered. "I'm only trying to be safer. We'll need to pull these ourselves, I think. All the pictures have..." She stared at the screen, flipped back and forth, reading labels. "They have horses and cows and things to pull them. We'll need people to do it. Unless you have a horse in your back pocket?"

He frowned, rubbing the stump of his left thumb absently. "I don't suppose you can harness the demon dogs or the djuri?"

She laughed. "The demons are too mean and the djuri are too frightened and the hebras are too tall. So we have to be able to pull it, at least for now."

"It will take more than one person to pull something that big. You'll have to make it smaller. Maybe it can have two wheels? And be thinner?"

She frowned. "Maybe."

"It would still be heavy."

Joy tightened her jaw and sat back, but then said, "We don't need to take it everywhere. Just to the ends of the roads. Like today, where we set up a camp and explore from there."

"I hope someone lets you make it." With that helpful comment, Johannes resumed his slow circuit through the library, quieting children and helping people find obscure information about plants or animals in the growing Fremont database. She glared at his retreating back. None of the first colonists understood. Fremont might kill them all. They were used to being on top, back on Deerfly. They'd fled other humans, but for all she could tell, every animal on Deerfly had been domesticated.

On Fremont, humans weren't the apex predator. At least not yet.

She turned back to her notes, and before she knew it, the sky had darkened into night. Johannes started rattling the doors, breaking her concentration. She looked up to find that she was the only one left except Johannes.

"I'm sorry."

He smiled at her. "Good luck with the wagon. It might work."

"Thanks." She picked up her notebook and hurried outside, looking up to see a sky spangled with stars. She spotted Destiny, and then two other moons. A good luck sign.

The gathering bells began to toll just before dusk. Joy didn't want to go, but the ritual ran deep. Everyone who knew the dead went to every funeral. She had been with Bart when he died, so she'd have a place in the ceremony because of that. She pulled on dark pants and her best white shirt and combed her hair, then sat to wait for her mother.

The bells had already stopped by the time her mother showed up, dressed in an old black shirt of Joy's father's. Her hair hung in dark waves streaked with gray. The flour had been scrubbed from her face and hands.

She walked beside Joy with her eyes downcast. She had hardly said a thing to Joy these three days, and Deborah had told Joy that she seldom spoke to anyone else either. She tottered a bit on her feet. Joy supported her, wondering if she had been drinking the colony's homemade alcohol. It went unsaid between them, but drinking was part of why her mother never went out any more, and why Deborah provided for most things that Joy needed.

Joy took her mother's hand. "Can you move a little faster?"

Her mother shook her head but made a visible effort. When Joy's father died, she had been seven. Joy had wished it was her and not him, her mother and not him, anyone in the colony *but* him. Her mother had not recovered.

She swallowed and squeezed her mother's hand. Of course, she hadn't recovered. Joy's father had been perfect. He'd been the lead biologist, and the way her mother talked, he'd been the most handsome man in the whole colony. "It will be okay," she murmured, as much to herself as to her mother.

"It's *not* okay," he mother whispered. "Another death. We'll all be gone."

Joy held on to her mother's sweaty hand and kept walking toward the funeral clearing.

They were almost the last to arrive. One of the Council members, Lucille, came and took Joy's hand and led her to the front of the procession, separating her from her mother. Joy breathed out a sigh of relief and took her place. Lucille led them in a circle. Three Council members were first, then Deborah as the lead scientist, then Joy as speaker for the last sight.

Lucille stopped and the others followed, lining up close to each other at the head of the pyre. The other mourners stood at the foot in a loose bunch that stretched far back. Hundreds of people, but still fewer than had landed here. Even with the babies. A cool breeze brushed stray strands of hair from her face as she took a deep breath. Her hands shook just like her mother's often did.

Lucille lit the torch that would light the fire and held it blazing in her hand. The light deepened the lines in her face so she looked old and fierce.

Now that Joy stood where she could see Bart's shrouded body, she realized she had no idea what to say. She had never had this role. Her mother had been the last to see her father alive. Joy didn't remember what she had said.

As Lucille said her piece representing the colony, Joy's mind jumped back and forth through all the times she had seen Bart. She had not liked him, and she was angry with him for letting the fire die down. For almost killing her. For dying. But she couldn't say any of those things.

Lucille finished too fast for Joy's taste, and Deborah began to speak. "Bart was one of the last three working scientists from among the original colonists. I am another one. We have seen twenty-two die natural deaths, seventeen die in the field, and ten have been so wounded they entered the colony's service as part of the Culture Guild. Bart journeyed far to get here, to save us from a life we did not want. Little did he—or we—know that this place we fled to would kill so many of us. But he never flinched."

Deborah flicked her eyes toward Joy.

That glance burned into her as Deborah continued, "He travelled out to find us knowledge fifty-three times." She hesitated, as if she wanted to say something more. But she simply finished with, "We should all honor his service," and bowed her head.

The crowd murmured.

A lump clogged Joy's throat. She still had no idea what to say, even though she had heard the ritual over and over. Still, she *had* to talk. It was *her job* to relate his last night. "We stopped. Our last night's stop of a four-day trip. We had two tents and one fire and we watched the fire together until Bart felt we might run out of wood. Then he sent me to bed in my tent. After the fire died, so did he." That wasn't enough. She wiped at an unexpected tear. "A paw-cat came into camp and took his life." Her anger with Bart started to drain away. Something else came up in its place, a feeling she couldn't quite name yet, if ever. "We must do better." Her voice rose. "We must find a way to beat those things, to be safer and braver. We must act differently in order to live." She thought of her idea from today. "We must travel differently, travel in bigger groups, and make safety more important. There were supposed to be two other people with me and Bart, but Danny got sick so Carla stayed with him, and we started home anyway. We shouldn't have." The words startled her and she stopped for a moment, gazing across the waiting pyre at the watchers. "We need to be more afraid and to be let that fear make us stronger." She and the other scientists her age had said these things to each other. But none of them had said them to the colony.

Joy shook herself. This was no time for a lecture, but she'd had to say what she'd said. It had demanded to come out. She held her head up. "We are one colony. No one else is coming after us. Every one of us matters. Bart mattered. Bart was not afraid. But every death diminishes us." And now, finally, she remembered what she was expected to say, and the ritual took its proper cadence. "His last moments were spent protecting us all. May his soul fly free."

Lucille nodded and set her torch to the dried moss that would fire the kindling.

As she watched the pyre, Joy realized she would miss Bart even though she hadn't liked him. She whispered the words she'd said out loud. "We must act differently in order to live." Her expectation had been to die. Her mother thought that, and she had thought it too. That they would all die. Not of old age, but of this damned planet.

The next morning, Joy stood just outside Deborah's door fifteen minutes before the shift was supposed to start. Deborah opened the door, one hand full of an empty teacup and the other holding a notebook. She looked slightly irritated when she saw it was Joy, but then her face softened in non-committal kindness. "Did you come to tell me you're ready to go out?"

"Give me three people and three days. Please."

"Three? For what?"

"We're going to make wheels."

"Wheels?"

"Like on our bicycles. Like the little ones on the push-carts in the guild hall, but bigger."

"Out of metal?"

Joy shook her head.

"How?" There was no manufacturing to speak of on Artistos. Not yet. There were plans, but mostly they made do with things they brought down from the ship. "We'll use the Carpenter Guild's woodshop."

Joy saw the word "no" forming on Deborah's lips. She whispered, "Please."

Deborah's mouth thinned into a straight line and then she turned her back on Joy and headed for her kitchen. "I'll be right there."

Joy stood, tapping her foot. She smelled redberry tea. Deborah didn't offer her any, but when she came back, she said, "Two days. I'll be out that long bringing the things back from your camp."

Joy looked away. She should go with Deborah, but she couldn't face the camp. She really couldn't. "Thank you."

"You can choose three helpers from the culture guild."

From the old and the broken. Three days wouldn't have been enough, and two wouldn't be for sure. Not with the culture guild for her only help. Cripples and failures and the old. People like her mother. But she'd take two days without leaving the perimeter and two days to think about a safe place to sleep.

She didn't even know who all was in the culture guild. A few. But she was in the science guild, and she knew the ones that helped them. Johannes, for example.

She found him washing the windows in the science guild hall. He smiled at her. "Back for more?"

She clasped her hands behind her back and smiled at him. "Yes. They gave me permission. I have two days. And I can use three people to help me."

He blinked at her.

She felt her cheeks get hot. "Will you help me?"

"Me? Why not use builders or scientists?"

"I can't. Deborah said I can do this, but she said I need to use people from the Culture Guild."

He swallowed and took a breath before he answered her. "I have to do this." He pointed at the windows. "We all have jobs."

She stared at him. A clean window was more important than saving scientist's lives?

He flinched, and then said, "I can help you at the end of my shift."

Half her time would be gone. "You're one of the best. You know how to look up information. Please."

Johannes glanced at the computers. "What will the children do for classes?"

Her mind stumbled over ideas. "Can someone else help them today?"

He merely pursed his lips.

"Can they help us? Do they need to learn search skills? Can they apply those in class today? You helped me figure out that wheels can be made of wood. They did that on Earth, before we knew how to make metal. We could make heavy ones out of big circles, but then we couldn't pull them up hills. Can your class look up how to make them lighter? Then how to put them on axels?"

He narrowed his eyes at her. "The whole thing made of wood?"

Desperation threatened to wrap itself around her tongue. He had to help her. She couldn't fail. Not now. "Or things we have now. I want to build one in two days. And they have to be safe and have a locked place to sleep that's not on the ground and a way for there to be a fire."

"That's a lot to ask."

"I'm tired of people dying."

"What if, in two days, we get a good drawing?"

She swallowed, remembering lying in the tent, remembering the way the cat's claws sounded as it dragged Bart away, remembering that there had been nothing she could do. She didn't want the same to happen again, ever. "I want a good wagon. We have to at least try."

Johannes held up his thumbless hand. "I'm no good at building."

She held up her hands, fingers splayed. "We'll have enough thumbs."

He smiled at her, the first real, genuine smile she'd seen on another human being all day.

Johannes helped her choose two other people to include, a slightly-stooped man named Roke who used to work in the engine rooms of *Traveler,* the ship they'd flown here on, and a teenage boy named Pillat who had been born with one twisted leg. Pillat was the only human to start life out in the Culture Guild rather than enter it after they got too old, too sick, too frightened, or too injured to do the harder work of colonizing a dangerous planet. Joy was a little skeptical of both choices until they began the work, sitting all together around a table with two computers and a few pieces of paper between them all.

Pillat could only take a few steps on his own, but he had a wheeled chair he used to go between buildings. He was fast. He brought them water, food, and a few times, people Roke wanted to question. People came. That was Roke's magic; everyone knew him, and more importantly, trusted him. She'd seen him, of course, but she hadn't really known a thing about him. When he sent Pillat to ask a question, people responded. Every time. So Roke brought resources and respect as well as his own engineering knowledge, Pillat acted as a runner, Johannes researched, and Joy used her knowledge of the world beyond the boundary to drive the design.

By midday, Joy realized this was the best day she'd had in a long time.

Johannes periodically came in from his class with images and ideas and questions.

By nightfall they had a list of materials, a set of drawings, tools they'd sent Pillat to gather from various places, and four exhausted smiles. They also had three or four things they needed but didn't know how to get, including the metal rims that they wanted. And this was just for the wheels. There hadn't been time to design the living quarters, other than as a hand-drawn box with a hand-drawn window in the side and the outline of two doors.

Still, the small pile of tools encouraged her. They looked hopeful all laid out on the counter, like they were just waiting to be picked up.

They sat together and kept talking while they dipped djuri stew from the communal dinner pot. After they ate, Joy wanted to keep working, but Pillat had fallen asleep right on the dining room table and Johannes kept rubbing his eyes. So she thanked them all and went to her own room.

Once there, all of her good energy crashed around her. They had nothing yet. Just an idea. And only one more day.

Johannes had asked her what would happen if they only had a drawing. She knew. Deborah would make her go back out, and they'd keep doing things the same old way.

Joy slept fitfully, waking so early she could spot the bright light of *Traveler* in the sky near the horizon. She walked into the Science Guild just after dawn and found Roke already there, his work-roughened hands swirling a sanding stick across a long round of wood. He smiled when she walked in, held out the wood.

She took it. When she cupped one end in her palm, the other end extended behind that same elbow. It felt good. Heavier than she wanted, but also right. Solid.

"It's a spoke. So that's almost half as long as the first wheel will be high."

"Thank you," she told him, carefully handing him back the wood. "Thank you for working on it last night."

He resumed his sanding. "Mickey has nine more of these ready. He's going to do more after his shift ends."

After his shift ended? "Who's Mickey?"

"He's a carpenter. He's got a bad leg, so he's one of us in a way, but during the day he's one of the crew building the barn."

She had known the Science Guild worked dawn to dusk. What if everyone worked this hard and the colony still died off? "Tell him thank you." She sat down on a chair. "This isn't going to be finished in a day, is it?"

He looked at her with a wry smile. "Did you think it would?"

She bit her lip to keep back tears of frustration. "I'd hoped. At least for the wheels."

"Why don't you keep designing the living quarters?"

Pillat came in before she could fall any closer to despair, and his smile was so bright that she dug out the papers they had been working on and started making lists of things that might matter about a mobile house.

The others had gone off to various chores associated with the project, so Joy sat alone at the work table, staring at the papers spread across it and making small notes. As the golden light of dusk pierced the still-dirty windows of the science guild, Deborah threw the door open and came in to stand beside Joy. "What have you finished?"

Joy took a deep breath and tapped the paper in front of her. "Sit down and I'll show you." Deborah took a seat and Joy paged through their notes and drawings, some in her slightly sloppy hand, some in Pillat's rounded, extravagant style, and some in Johannes' neat block letters and squared images.

Deborah sat beside Joy and looked at the pictures and documents. "Can the wheels be made?"

"Roke has started on a sample wheel."

Deborah's eyebrows rose. "Is it done?"

Joy swallowed. "It's started. I think he'll be by with it. We also figured out the axle. The science students helped."

"Do we have strong enough wood for the axle?"

"Yes. We might even have metal parts we can use. There's a whole pile of recycled metal behind the Carpenter's Hall. Leftovers, or things that have come down that no one knew what to do with. We're asking."

"How many people will it take to pull?"

Joy swallowed. This was a hard one. "I think two. Except up hills. And it depends on how much is being carried. We'll have to stay on the roads with it, and build more, I suppose. But we usually camp near the roads anyway."

Deborah frowned. "We carry everything on our backs now. We could still carry things up hill. But could you pull this and carry your pack?"

"We hope so. It's more to make a safe place to sleep than to carry things, but it will carry things on the flats and it will be a safe place to leave things while we explore."

Deborah gave a light nod at that. Not exactly encouragement, but Joy knew it was a good point. Just last year they'd had a camp ravaged and a tent destroyed. She kept grilling Joy. "Do you have enough planed wood for the walls? That isn't needed for anything else? Like the barns?"

This was a much harder question, and not one she could answer. "The Town Council would have to say."

Deborah smiled as if Joy had answered something right. "How long will it take to build a sample?"

Before Joy could answer, the door opened and Pillat darted through it, quick in his chair, holding the door open. "Joy?"

"Here." Joy stood up. "Deborah is here, too."

Pillat glanced at Deborah, and hesitated a second before saying, "That's good. She can see, too. Come look!"

The boy sounded triumphant, but even more importantly, Deborah smiled broadly at him, and said, "You look better than I've seen you in years."

Pillat was nearly bouncing in his seat. "Wait until you see."

Outside, Roke stood beside a single wheel, his arm extended to hold it up. It was as tall as Pillat in his chair, which was bigger than she had expected. Joy practically skipped to the wheel. With that, the floor of the wagon would be higher than her knees. It would cross over good-sized rocks and handle tough terrain. She reached out to touch it. The wood was smooth and strong, and now that she was close, she could see a metal band around the outside edge. It was so strong.

Roke beamed at her. "Roll it." He let go.

She gasped as she caught it, surprised by how light it felt. It leaned a little toward her, and when she pushed it the other way it leaned a little too far, but Roke put a hand out and stopped it. She steadied herself and turned toward the wheel, using her hands and shuffling her feet to take it a full rotation. It moved so smoothly!

She had forgotten about Deborah until she realized she had to stop the wheel to avoid running into the head scientist.

Deborah's eyes were wide, but her expression otherwise showed no emotion.

Joy swallowed, suddenly afraid. It was only one part. One wheel. They needed four and the wagon itself, but she was out of time.

Deborah reached her hand out close to the wheel and waited for Joy to push it toward her. Joy didn't want to let go of it, but she did, stepping back beside Pillat and Roke.

Johannes came around the corner and stood watching the scene, his face as impassive at Deborah's.

Why did Deborah have to come now? The four of them should have been able to examine the wheel before they had to share it with someone as skeptical as Deborah.

The older woman moved the wheel gingerly forward and back, and then squatted, attempting to pick it up. She held it, her arms quivering a bit with the weight. She and wheel made a long shadow on the ground, almost comical in the late-evening light. The metal rim turned a burnished orange. Deborah stood there, holding the wheel, looking away from all of them.

Joy bit her lip. It was heavier than she wanted. But it had the metal rim, which was a good idea. The wheel would last a lot longer.

Deborah put the wheel down carefully, still on its edge, and rolled it over to the building. She leaned it there and backed up, staring at it. She stopped when she was close to Joy, Roke, and Pillat. Johannes came over near them.

Deborah gestured for them all to go back into the guild. Deborah led, and Joy chose to go in last, stopping for a moment to touch the wheel before darting in through the door. This was physical, demonstrable proof that her ideas could work. The scientists could travel more safely.

After they all sat down, Johannes lit a candle against the fading light.

Deborah gave him a strange look, and he shrugged his shoulders as if to shake it off. "Another breaker blew this afternoon.

I'll fix it first thing in the morning. We're getting low on electrical wire, though, and may need another trip to *Traveler*."

Deborah's expression soured at that, but she nodded at Roke. "That's good work. How many people helped?"

"Just me and Mickey. We skipped dinner to finish it." He glanced at the wheelchair-bound boy. "And Pillat. He brought us things we needed and picked up after us."

At that, Deborah smiled.

Johannes stood and went to the kitchen, bringing back a tray with a pitcher of water and five cups on it.

Joy sipped at her water, watching Deborah's face carefully. The Culture Guild didn't report to the head of the Science Guild, but half its members had once been scientists. Deborah would be able to stop their project if she wanted to.

Instead, Deborah looked at Roke and asked, "How long will it take to build an entire mockup?"

Roke and Johannes shared a glance, while Pillat looked to Joy as if she had been asked the question.

She hadn't. Which made her tighten her muscles into a fake grin. She forced herself to take a deep breath and blow out her anger. It wouldn't help. Thinking might. It had only taken two days to design and build one wheel. How long would it take to build more now that they had the design? Three more days for the insides of the wagon? Maybe not ready to live in, but ready to test? She could practically see the same ideas turning over Roke's head. She pushed her anger with Deborah to the side, for now. "Can we get three wheels in two more days? Are there enough materials?"

Roke smiled. "Three days for sure. If we have to do it after our other work." He nodded toward Deborah, who still said nothing. He pursed his lips at her silence, and then turned his attention back to Joy. "Can you finish designing the kitchen? I think if we tape off the size on the floor and use physical things— maybe boxes and old wood—to measure with, you'll see how big it is. I think you might be able to add three drawers."

Deborah stood, as if she had finally made a decision. "As much as I might later regret letting a man do it, you will have to design the kitchen. And if you want to do this, you must do it after hours, and you must have the other Guilds working with you. We can't afford to waste the good weather that's coming next week, so Joy, you'll be in the field with me and three other apprentice scientists." She hesitated. "Plus a few more who are more seasoned. It will be a big enough group for safety. We'll be looking for more species of berries to test and we'll try to catch more jumping prickles."

Joy swallowed a lump in her throat. She had truly enjoyed the last two days, and now she'd be sent out to face Fremont again.

Deborah continued. "We'll be gone for two weeks. Can you finish in that time?"

Roke nodded, pointedly not looking at either Joy or Deborah. Pillat rolled over close to Joy, the sad smile on his lips suggesting he understood a little of what she felt. Johannes's face was still. On all of those faces, and in her own heart, she felt the depth of Deborah's power like a rock crushing their ability to choose anything for themselves. She stood abruptly, offering Deborah a stiff little bow. "Thank you for allowing my work to continue."

She turned and walked out the building, grateful that the darkness was sufficient to hide her angry tears.

To her surprise, she found her mother sitting on a rock outside of the scientists' quarters, barely visible in the pale stored-solar light that marked the way to the shared bunk space that included her room. She hadn't seen her mother since they walked to the funeral together. As soon as Joy saw her, her mother stood and came to greet her. "I heard what you said."

"Huh?"

"You said we had to change and we had to do better."

Joy ran her hands down her cheeks, trying to remove any evidence of her tears. "We do. That's why I'm trying to build a safer way to be out there."

Joy's mom smiled. "And why I'm going back out. I asked Deborah if I could go with you. I know how to test the berries, and I can cook for all of you." She looked directly at Joy, and her gaze was calmer and more resolute than Joy had seen it in years.

Her mom was going to go *now*?

Joy took her mom's hands. They shook, in spite of how calm she looked. "What did Deborah say?"

"She said yes."

"That's good." She wanted to tell her mom how grateful she was. How it was almost a motherly thing, wanting to go with Joy after that last horrible trip. "Maybe, if it works out, we'll have a place you can cook more easily in the fall." She gestured for her mother to sit back down on the rock and she sat beside her. Joy still didn't want to go through the boundary, but she would do it to be beside her mom. She told her mom about the wagons, and about the perfect wheel.

Night birds began to call from the trees between buildings. Above their heads, the sky filled with stars. Joy took her mom's hand in hers again, and this time it didn't shake. Deborah always made sure there was no alcohol outside the boundaries. Maybe this was a way forward. And after working with Roke, Johannes, and Pillat for two days, Joy was sure they'd make a wagon. She leaned close to her mom and rested her head on her mom's shoulder. It felt like a safe spot, a safe moment. She breathed in spices and flour and oil that clung to her mother, and beyond those, the various spicy and rich scents of the wild planet.

Fremont might never be truly safe, but maybe they could build more safe spots and safe moments.

The Hebras and the Demons and the Damned

Brenda Cooper

I'm going to ramble a bit. Let me; I'm no roamer speaking over a communal fire. I'm not sure I know which parts of the story you want. But this is part of how Fremont was saved and kind of an alien contact story, too.

My name is Chaunce, and I am one of the few left on Fremont who remembers the home we left behind. Deerfly. Stupid name for a planet, if you ask me. But we didn't leave Deerfly over its wreck of a name. Rather, it was too smart for us, everybody there becoming stronger, faster beings, almost becoming computers or robots with flesh, leaving us true humans behind, some of them wearing no more than a thin skin of flesh to fool the eye.

Fremont was too smart for us, too. In the time I'm telling you about, we'd been here seventeen years. Instead of doing what a self-respecting colony does and growing, we kept losing people to tooth and claw and cliff.

Real humans had grown up on colony planets like this, but Deerfly had gone tame generations ago.

We needed help. Needed to find some accord with this place before it killed us. It gnawed at me that I'd done so little for the colony except back-breaking work and staying alive. I'd left the leading to others, and Fremont needed more from me than that. Since I managed horse farms back on Deerfly, I looked to the animals.

Now, there are a lot of animals on Fremont, but most wouldn't work for what I needed.

The cats had decided we were dinner the day we landed, and they were too big to be undecided in any way I could think of. A foot-long scar on my right calf throbbed in the cold of winter; a reminder.

We had a few domestic dogs we'd brought shipboard and more we were planning to birth and raise up. We weren't going to lack for best friends, for herding beasts to keep goats in bunches, or four-footed pranksters to steal the chickens. But dogs are smaller than humans, and smaller than most beings of tooth and claw here. I was glad of them, but on Fremont they needed protecting just like we did. They'd give us warning, but they'd die trying to save us from paw cats or yellow snakes. And given how we mostly loved them, humans sometimes died saving their dogs.

Fremont has its own four-footed and single-tailed beasts with a canine look. They run in packs, and people call them demon dogs. But they should never, ever be confused for real dogs. These demons have no soul, and they exist to eat. Worse, I've seen them hunt, and I'm sure they are communicating with each other more than any of our native animals from Deerfly, or the ones our fathers brought from Earth. Demons don't speak, but they work like a team with radios. They make humans mildly sick to eat, too. So they're not even good for food.

I had high hopes for the djuri: four-footed prey that run in packs, fleeing for their lives from the demon dogs. It turned out the djuri were too shy to help. Hard to find, always running and hiding and bleating. Not too bright, either, and not big enough to really help us. Humans can look down on them, or maybe look a big one straight in the eye. Well, all right. A few are even bigger than that. The bucks. But still, they're not hefty creatures. Keep in mind that we can look a paw cat in the eye, too, and they outweigh us and have claws as long as fingers and hard as knives. The truly good thing about djuri is they are incredibly good to eat.

That's pretty much the rundown on the bigger animals we'd seen here so far, except the hebras. They were our last hope for an answer. I took a while to realize this, even though I sat at the edge of the cliff by the promise of our town, looking down over the grass plains every day for two summers. The grass there is scary big, bigger than a man's head by the end of summer. When it dries, it's sharp like a million razors trying to flay the skin from anything as soft as a human. I still have scars on my fingers from it, and on my shoulders.

As tall as the grass is, the hebras' heads rise above it. They've got legs that come to a man's head. Instead of straight backs like horses, their backs slope up to shoulders, and their necks measure the tiniest bit longer than their backs. Their coats are solid, striped, or are covered with great spots like the shadow pattern of leaves on the forest floor. Their colors are all variation of gold and green, brown and black, and sometimes the barest bit of red like a red-haired woman being touched by the sun.

Make no mistake. Hebras are prey animals. Paw cats hunt them all summer, and demons get the weak and the slow and the young. But they are so much more. Remember how I told you about the demon dogs? Perhaps being prey on a planet full of thorns made them smarter than any of the horses I ever rode or trained or showed or loved.

One day, far below me, the demon dogs hunted hebras. I'd given up digging out the smelter's foundation for the day, my muscles screaming sore and my back feeling on fire. I stood at the edge of the cliff looking down, letting the cooling breeze of near-dusk tease sweat from my skin. The sun shone bright enough to wash everything dull and soft, with that little extra bit of gold that the late part of the day brings. The air smelled of seeds and harvest and of the fall that would soon touch us.

Below me a herd of hebras grazed, rotating between watcher and eater, the distance making animals with heads towering above my own look small.

A breeze kissed the tops of the grasses, bending them south in ripples. A few lines of grass moved the wrong way as a pack of seven demons surrounded twice as many hebras. I spotted the dogs' path even before the wily old watch-hebra bugled fear and loathing.

The hebras ran together, almost lockstep, all of them trying for a gap between two of the demons, heading sideways to me, their heads bobbing up and down with their ungainly rocking run.

The dogs raced to make a line in front of the hebras, cutting them off. They began to bay, a high long-winded howl that instilled fear in me, even though I stood so far above them the sound was faint and thin.

The hebras turned, all together, a wave of long necks and thin tails.

The dogs flowed behind them.

The tallest hebra let out a short high-pitched squeal and the hebras twitched and broke into three lines, making one-hundred-and-eighty degree turns as if they practiced every day. Maybe they did. They had it down, stretching out long, taking turns teasing the dogs. The gap between grazer and hunter widened.

A dog nipped at the last animal in one line, a brown blur flashing momentarily up above the high grass and then falling back down. The target hebra twisted, probably kicking, even though I couldn't see its legs for the grass, and then put on a burst of speed. It passed two other hebras, and a different animal became last, running right in front of the slavering dogs.

I'd been in the grass the week before. It pulled and cloyed and knotted and tripped. But the hebras and the demons slid through it, streams of living beings, barking and baying and bugling.

The air had cooled down a little, but I stood with goosebumps rising on my forearms, transfixed, and afraid that if I moved I'd somehow change the outcome of the race down below.

It was nearly too dark to see by the time the first of the dogs stopped, the grass swallowing the hunter as it became still. I lost the place it stood entirely in the space of two breaths.

As the stars and two of our moons brightened in the black sky above me, I realized the hebras had won fairly easily. They were off grazing somewhere else, and the dogs would have a hungry night.

If it had been fourteen unarmed humans against seven demons, I'd have bet on the dogs.

Our roving scientists brought back a lot of djuri bones; jaws and the think back leg bones cracked open by teeth. But not many hebra bones. Some. They did die. But not very fast, or very easy.

So I swore I'd figure out how to tame them. Not that we'd gotten within two hundred meters by then. The great beasts were shy of us, and fast.

I couldn't catch one myself. I was almost sixty already, and slowing. I took my story to the Town Council, which was led by Jove Alma at the time, a nervous man with a deep focus on making and keeping plans. He thought the tighter he gripped our choices in his and the Council's fist, the more of us would live. Some believed him, some hated him, but everyone obeyed. The previous leader had taken risks, and cost almost all of us people we loved. That's the long way 'round of saying that catching animals wasn't in Jove's plan, and the Council turned me down flat. There was a city being built and the chill of winter already clinging to every dawn.

The winter was the second harshest we'd ever had, with snow in town, instead of just in the hills, and two sheet-ice storms. We lost ten more people. Two froze to death on a trip out into the woods to bring back samples of winter plants, leaving behind two orphans to add to our growing stockpile. The third one who went with them lost three fingers and part of her sanity. Cats ate two adults and a babe, fire claimed a family of four and one of the men my age hanged himself in the middle of town. We had two less births than deaths that season.

All that long cold season I thought of the hebras. Sometimes I glimpsed them down below on the cold grass plains. Fire had flamed the grass flat and low and the hebras sometimes loped like shadows at the edge of the plain near the sea, clearly visible when frost turned the stubble white and hoary in the early dawn. But mostly they hid in the Lace Forest that surrounded us.

Come spring, we stopped huddling together in the buildings we'd made for guild halls and finished up some of the houses. I built mine at the edge of town, as close to the cliff as the Town Council would let me. Mornings, as dawn split the sky open, I sat and watched the fading moons and the greening grass below. The hebras returned, sleeping on the plain, two watch beasts circling the sleepers restlessly, heads way up. I was pretty sure they traded off watches just like we did, and for the same reason. It made me feel kindred.

One morning when the grass was knee-high to a human and the first spindly-legged baby hebras clung to their dams, Jove came and stood silently beside me, looking down at the plains. His gaze was unfocused, as if he saw the whole thing and the sea beyond, but not the hebras right below. "Three of the orphans got in trouble last night. Fought each other and one's fetched up in the infirmary with a broken leg."

He'd hate that. Jove hated all disorder. I waited him out, curious what he'd say next.

"Council met, and we figure you got room for two boys."

Shock gave way to liking the idea pretty fast. I'd never married, never had kids, just managed farms and hired help. But there was no help to hire here. My ancestors had farmed Deerfly by making babies, back in the days before there were too many bots and androids to count and people didn't have any work to do that looked like farming except training exotics. So I didn't stand and blink stupidly at Jove for long, but instead I just said, "Thank you."

He looked surprised at that, like he'd been expecting resistance, so it was his turn to pause for a beat too long and then say, "Thank you," himself. He smiled before he walked away, the sun fully risen now, shoving his shadow behind him as he walked back to town.

The boys were Derk and Sho. Derk was thin and wiry, and won the boys' informal footraces. Sho plodded, and had so much patience I couldn't imagine what had made him part of the fight at all until one day I came across two other boys teasing him in high, mean voices for being stupid. They were wrong; I already knew that. But sometimes being the silent type means people make their own decisions about who you are.

Sho and Derk had school and then work every day, but since they were only twelve, they had energy to spare in spite of the harsh schedules. It only took a few days before they stood beside me at the cliff's edge, looking down at the herd.

Sho started drawing hebras in the dirt with sticks and they both started naming them.

As the days got longer, we gave up sleep to pick our way down the steep path between Artistos and the wide road on the plains where we'd trucked tools and technology from the shuttles at our makeshift spaceport.

The boy with the broken leg, Niko, recovered enough to follow us down the path and soon all three of them laughed together, their raised voices surely spreading all across the plain. Soon half the teens and a few of the old singles from town began to join us at the crack of dawn.

Some of the watchers wanted to catch a hebra, some to stun one. Those weren't the right answers. I knew it deep in my gut, found it hard to say why I knew so hard, so I just told them, "If we scare them off, they might never come back." I never let them get close to the herds, just to watch them. The boys helped me— all three of them now living with me, and acting like herd dogs to the new people.

The trail from town to plain lay nearly naked against the cliff, a thin ribbon of dirt with no place big enough for predators to hide. We could stand safely or sit on small rocks and talk. The hebras knew we were there, sometimes lifting their heads and pointing their broad, bearded faces at us. I wanted them to know we weren't their enemy. We kept it up all summer, the crowd straining against my calls for patience. Sho stood beside me, facing them, telling them off with his eyes and his stance, and they listened. Derk and Niko stood quietly at the rear, watching everyone and all the hebras, eyes darting from one to one to one, keeping count and order.

Some of the boys were fascinated with the hebras' beards, maybe because they had the first hint of stubble on their own chins. They started drawing pictures of the girls in town with beards and longish necks, and giggling.

The grass stretched its fairy-duster seed-pods toward the autumn sky, tall as me if I stood inside it. Demons started hunting more, sometimes running the hebras twice a day. The herd lost one old hebra and one very young one that twisted a leg. The pack lost one old dog and two pups. So in a way, the hebras were winning. Except of course that one hebra fed all the dogs and dead dogs didn't feed the hebras anything.

The cats stayed away. I suspect our scent and presence did that. They hunted us as quickly as hebra, but they liked us in small groups. There were about twenty humans on the path most mornings.

Once a week or so Jove came and watched, always walking away before the bells rang for breakfast. I knew that he was thinking, but it did no good to push Jove, and thus no good to push the Town Council. But if the plains burned below us, we'd have to wait another year to capture even one hebra.

One morning after Jove ghosted away from us, Sho asked, "Is he scared of catching one?"

"Hard work to run a colony. He has to choose."

"He should see how much we and the hebras need each other."

I suspected the boy had the right of it, but it does no good to downtalk leaders. "Jove is a busy man."

"Can you ask him for some rope?"

"What are you going to do with rope?"

"Catch a hebra."

"Probably not. You think about how to do that, and we'll try your idea if I can get rope. Rope is dear." We had what we'd brought, and some we'd made. But none of our homemade rope was strong enough for this.

"Please ask."

The persistence of boys. "If an opening comes up."

About noon that same day, Jove came by to watch us raise the roof on the smelter. The metal slabs had come all the way from Deerfly and been brought in pieces from *Traveler* in one of the little shuttles a year ago. Jove stood to the side as we used chain to hoist the metal, the chain travelling over a tall wooden post-and-beam structure we'd lashed together just for this job. Even with the leverage it took three men sweating to get the last and largest section up and held, while three more of us fastened it with nails also brought from the ship.

At the end, Jove came and stood silently beside me. "Good job, Chaunce. Now we can make our own nails."

"That's what we did all this work for? Nails?"

"And hinges. And maybe bits for those animals down below." He nodded at the roof. "One of your beasts might have pulled that easier."

It wasn't a use I had thought of—I'd been thinking of riding them. I felt doubtful they'd be pullers. But if they were—we could make wagons and flatbeds and farm tools. The thought was good. "Can I have some rope?"

"You might get hurt. Or die. The boys might die."

"We've gotta find accord with some of the wild things here. We can't fear them all forever." But then, he'd lost a wife to a pack of demons, found her in pieces three days after we landed. Years had passed, but some memories burn your soul.

He toed the ground for a while.

I could get enough Council to override him if I really tried. But he was a good leader, and I'd learned that if you undermine a good leader you can be rewarded with a worse one.

He swallowed and looked off at some distant spot in the sky before he said, "Let's go get it."

I had plenty of time to think, lurching home in the darkening night with three hundred feet of rope coiled over my right shoulder. I understood Jove's issue: time breathed down on us. We were failing, dying by bits each year as we missed goals, became food for the local predators, fought amongst each other, and tried ever so hard to learn the dangers and opportunities here. We needed more stout, warm buildings, to retrieve the rest of our supplies from *Traveler* before the shuttles ran out of fuel, to build better perimeters, and to breed more children than Fremont took from us. Taking the three boys out on the plains represented a hefty risk of our future. Better to risk boys than girls, but still...

When I dropped my load of rope on the ground outside the house, the three of them tumbled out right away, faces full of excitement. They'd been planning. Sho came up to me and said, "We can't get that over their heads. We can't get it around their legs or we might break them."

I considered. I'd been thinking of horses. But we were not cowboys. I'd never tried to catch a wild animal in my life. Ran from a few—here. The animals on my farms had been born in warm stables and grown up unafraid of me. This was a puzzle. "We can't cut the rope too short or we'll never be able to use it for anything else."

So we made walls on two sides, using the cliff as the other side.

We lost a whole day hiking to the Lace Forest and finding four big logs, dragging them back, and posting them upright into the ground. About the time we finished that, the work crews had broken for the day. They helped us string and tie the rope walls, the lowest rope at hebra-knee-height, which was about at our waists, and the highest something I could barely touch with my hands.

When we finished, the dark brown rope stood out against the pale green grasses of late autumn. The corral did not look like it would work for much of anything. Besides, I wasn't at all sure how we were going to get them anywhere near it.

Now we had to do what Jove was afraid of. We had to walk through the tall grass and get the hebras to walk away from us and into the makeshift corral. Maybe we shouldn't have done this—maybe we should have tried to get close without rope. Maybe we should have tried to find them in the winter woods. At any rate, it no longer mattered what we should have done. The shadow of night was knifing across the plains, and it was time to beat it up the cliff and bed down.

I slept fine, but before the first light all three boys came to my room. Derk, the biggest, rested his arms on Niko's and Sho's shoulders. "Sho was dreaming of hebras, and when he came to wake me up, I was dreaming about them, too."

Sho nodded. "We dreamed they got caught in the walls we made and the dogs got them, rising up over their back legs and standing on their backs." He stopped, his eyes wide. He might cry if I let him keep worrying, and then he'd lose face, and maybe be the next one to end up with a broken leg.

"And biting their necks." Niko added, not helping.

"Did you dream, too?" I asked Niko.

He shook his head. "No. But I'm worried about the hebras."

"Well, I'm glad you care. That should make it easier to catch them."

"Really?" Sho asked.

"Yes," I assured them all. Might as well believe in success. It couldn't hurt.

"Can we sit in here with you?" Niko asked.

So I let them stay. In ten minutes they had fallen asleep all over the bed like a litter of puppies, and I got up to watch for the light and make us all a good lunch. The apple trees had come in well this fall, and Jove's new wife, Maria, made excellent goat's milk cheese. We'd be set if we added a bit of fresh bread from the communal kitchen. Even though the morning shadows were still black ghosts, the first loaves should already be out. I shrugged into my coat and opened the door.

I nearly jumped as a shadow moved nearby. Jove. Wordlessly, he held out three loaves of bread.

"I don't need that many."

"Yes, you do. I gave everyone on your shift the day off."

I raised my eyebrows and spoke more boldly than I ever had to him. "Big risk for you."

Although I really only still had moonlight to see by, I swear his cheeks reddened. "I had trouble sleeping. I kept doing math in my head. Doing just what we're doing, if we keep dying so fast, there won't be anything left of us in two hundred years." He looked directly at me for the first time in a few days. "I remember what you said when you brought your ideas to us. Last year. We have to risk."

I could barely imagine what that cost him. People followed him because they were afraid. Like him. And now he was being brave. This would change us, and only success would change us for the better. The stakes had just risen.

Together, Jove and I made up sandwiches for thirty people. My shift-mates started gathering outside, stamping against the morning cold, dressed in layers against the heat that would follow by midday. They chattered amongst themselves, a few nervous, a few excited. Laughter broke out over and over.

The boys didn't want anything more than excitement for breakfast, but I got them each to take a bread heel down in their coat pockets against the hunger that would threaten them as soon as we stopped and waited. At first I worried that Jove would try to take over, although in truth, neither he nor I knew much of anything about hunting hebras.

He didn't take charge. He stood to the side, curious and watchful and very silent. People looked to him at first, and then when he looked to me, they did, too. A relief and a worry.

We handed out stunners to all of the adults, two to the good shots. Half of our total stock, a firepower that scared even me.

The stunners quieted everyone a bit. One shot would stop a human, two a demon, three a paw cat.

The hebra herd watched us come down, and of course, we watched them.

I expected them to think it was like any other morning, since we always came down with dawn to watch. But they scattered before we were even half-way down. Maybe because we started later than usual. Maybe just something in the way we walked, like we had a purpose instead of a simple curiosity.

Jove spoke what I was thinking. "Maybe they don't want us any more than the rest of this cursed planet wants us."

There were twenty-five of us total. I broke us into groups, and sent four groups of five off. I thought about keeping Jove with us, but since I was keeping all three boys I decided I needed a shooter I could count on, and so I sent Jove off with the group that I figured would be safest. So that's how me, the three boys, and my second-in-command from the smelter project, Campbell, all went over to stand downwind of the rope corral.

The boys ate some of their bread. Campbell and I watched, keeping companionable silence. The boys fidgeted. Campbell and I made them stretch in the grass, crawling and parting the fronds, reminding them to close their eyes and mouths as they moved through it, like swimmers. We sent them one by one up onto a small pile of rocks to look around the plain and see if they spotted the hebras (or anything else). They got bored and hungry and ate their bread heels and drank half the whole day's water supply. Derk got bit by something nasty and flying and a welt came up on his arm. He didn't complain, though. Good kid. It warmed and we stripped off our outer layer of coats.

The first group came in, including Jove. He shook his head at me. "Nothing."

The second and third groups found each other and came in together, then the fourth. No one reported seeing anything bigger than a jumping-prickle or a long-tailed rat. We made a long string of humans and sandwiches at the base of the cliff, still downwind from the ropes. We rested on warm rocks. The three boys abandoned me and Jove. I figured they'd be watched well enough between so many of us. Besides, they too had seen cats bring down a baby hebra this spring. Surely they'd be cautious.

"Did you see anything interesting out there?" I asked Jove.

"Grass."

Well, true enough. His right cheek showed a set of thin lines where he'd seen the grass too closely, and one had been deep enough that it was slightly crusted with blood.

"You should clean up before that starts itching." I dug an antiseptic cloth out of my bag, adding a bit of water from my canteen to bring it to life. Some plants here were the antidotes to other plants, and we had a whole team of botanists doing nothing more than cataloging everything we learned. This was one of their gifts. Jove took the cloth, and while he wiped up his cheek and a deeper cut I hadn't noticed on his forearm, I said, "They know we're here. They've been grazing here every day for two years except winters and today—maybe they're territorial and this is the territory for this herd. They've been watching us watch them, but they don't like us all the way down here."

"What next?" he asked.

We still had half of this day. "Let's try again today, send everyone in one group except me and Campbell and the boys. Have you all go together along the road so you get further away, and then make two teams and go forward. Maybe you can get far enough out for the hebras to be between you and me. Just don't spook them. Sometimes they sleep during the day, but they'll have watchers."

He handed me back the cloth instead of just putting it in his own pocket.

I took it.

"How do you know what they do during the day? You're always working."

"I ask around the fire at night. Almost no one sees them during the day. One theory suggests they go into the woods, another that they sleep when the big predators sleep. I kinda like—"

A scream cut my sentence off. One of the boys. "Demons!"

No! They slept during the day. I knew that. Everybody knew that. Damnit—What did I *know*? I leapt up, dropping the rest of my lunch, and scrambled to a higher rock behind me. Our line— stretched out maybe twenty meters—did the same, people backing up against the cliff.

"To me," I called. The demons would try and surround the ends first, to isolate a single person or two and then kill them easily. I tried to recall who was where, couldn't remember. Lousy leading.

A demon bayed as if answering me, the same call I'd heard from the cliff, shuddering. It was worse down here, and diffuse, like the wail came from all around, the grass and the plains themselves hunting us.

I couldn't tell where the demon was.

The boys.

Derk and Niko came running up to me, panting, standing one at each side of me, looking out. They trembled, but neither cried.

"Where's Sho?" I demanded, voice high and worried.

Another bay, and a yip. People gathered around us.

Derk found his breath. "Up. On the cliff."

Indeed, over the chaos of gathering, drawing stunners, screeching for each other, demons yipping and baying, I heard the high slip of Sho's voice.

I looked up.

He stood three meters above me, his feet dug into the cliff, apparently balanced on a ledge too small for me to see from below. He hung onto a tree growing thin and spindly out of dirt caught between rocks, leaning out. Close to falling. Now that I was looking at him, I could see he was screaming details. "Six of them. To the right."

I looked right. My head was above the grass, but barely. The stones we'd sat on made a small clearing, the grass close enough to throw shadows at our feet.

Sho would see them coming for us, but we wouldn't know until the grass parted in front of our faces.

The demon cries were still a bit away, but confident. Maybe the demons didn't care we were all together.

"One almost there!" Sho cried. "By you, Chaunce."

I raised my stunner, hand shaking. I'd fired at a demon once, missed as it came right at me fast as lightning. Louise had been behind me and she hadn't missed. Now the boys were behind me, small, no stunners.

The dog burst through the grass, long and sinewy, teeth bared, eyes black and full of hunger.

I fired.

Someone else fired.

The dog fell. Its coat rippled as another shot hit it.

"Stop!" I yelled. "Don't waste shots!"

"There!" Sho.

A second dog burst through in almost the same place, its body landing on the other one. This time we used four shots.

Derk pushed past me, knife in hand, bent on killing the stunned animals.

To my right, someone screamed, and in a moment of shock I heard the click of another stunner and another thump. Who screamed?

A hebra bugled, high and long. The same sound I'd heard a hundred times when this hunt played out below me and I merely watched.

"Back!" Sho screamed. The watch hebra. That's what Sho did for us.

Sho and a real hebra. What was the hebra doing here?

I backed up.

Derk ducked, his right hand now covered in demon blood.

A head rose above mine, above the grass, the neck long and thin, a white beard like my grandfather's last beard, long and thin.

I backed up faster.

The hebra passed between me and Derk in its lurching fast run, bigger than I expected, an animal the color of spring grass with gold spots on its knobby knees. It breathed deep and rattling but ran strong. A dog followed it, too fast for me to bring up my stunner.

The woman next to me, Paulette, screamed in joy, clapping.

"Watch!" Sho still sounded scared. "Stay back!"

More hebras, the whole herd of them, and dogs, all running together. The dogs had given up on us. They moved away a bit, the hebras now silent except for deep, sharp breathing, the dogs yipping and baying on their heels.

"Shoot the dogs!" I couldn't tell who yelled, the command a shiver down my spine.

Instinct told me. "No! The hebras can do this."

I stood as still as I could, the grass waving around me, the slick sounds of animals racing through it and the call and yips of hunter, hunted, and humans all distinct and all around.

A high-pitched squeal touched my heart. A hebra. I heard its body fall, a sound like a sack of flour thrown from the roof of a storage barn. Me and Jove and Campbell raced toward the fallen hebra. A dog passed right in front of me, its tail slapping me sideways. I raised my stunner and hit its flank.

It cried in pain, stopped, stood still, didn't fall.

I hit it again.

It mewled, sounded like a child needing help, like it didn't understand, and then it fell.

Ahead of me, the fallen hebra struggled up, blood dripping down its leg from a slash in its thigh. Shaking. Not broken.

Someone else dropped a dog to my right.

Two other hebras raced past us, screaming.

The few dogs left didn't draw off this time. They circled the beast that had just scrambled up. One of its knees bled.

There were four demons left. Few enough they should know better. Maybe the smell of blood drove them crazy.

Someone I couldn't see stunned another dog.

A dog I couldn't see let out a high, sharp bark and in heartbeats the pack was gone. They might have never been there, the grass closed across the memory of their hungry mouths and long, powerful legs.

The injured hebra took a step, and then another. Gingerly.

Two hebras walked through the grass, oblivious to us, and placed themselves on either side of the wounded one. One of the two strongest watch hebras came up to stand between me and the threesome, looking down at me. I stood there, craning my neck up, sweating, my ankle throbbing lightly from the side-step I'd taken. Its shoulder rose above my eye, its front knee about at my chest. Its fur looked coarser than I'd expected.

I kept my gun down.

If it could talk it would be telling me something with its calm gaze. Even though its sides heaved, it looked at me as if speaking sentences. They had no language we could understand, but they were at least as smart as the herding dogs. And some days I thought the collies were smarter than me. I knew I was in the presence of something good, even on this hellhole of a planet.

We would never capture such beasts in a rope corral. But they had allied themselves with us in that moment, voted with their thundering feet and high bugle calls. We would come to some kind of accommodation, some way to trade them safety for safety.

These are the things that went through my head as I watched the beast watch me.

The boys came up beside me and still the hebra watched, the plains silent now except for the ever-present buzz of instincts. It took a long time before the hebras moved off, stately, visible above the waving dry grass for a long time.

Fighting to Be Free

Danielle Ackley-McPhail

Unashamedly self
Resisting all efforts to subdue
Intrusion rebuffed
By tooth, and claw, and fang
Until the planet itself
Twitches and shakes
Then strikes out
Like a mother swatting
Misbehaving children

New Discoveries

Danielle Ackley-McPhail

Two hours before dawn Sala's pillow shook violently, accompanied by a faint buzzing sound barely loud enough to rouse just her. In truth, she had lain awake most of the night, waiting with anticipation for the time just before the guards changed shifts. In slow, sliding motions she'd practiced for weeks, she reached beneath the pillow to shut off the alarm before it could disturb her parents. As she drew her hand out she snagged the pouch she had hidden in her bed the previous night. It held a flask of water, nutrient bars, a med kit, and a collapsible bowl, along with its more precious cargo of specimen bags, graphite pencils, and parchment. Scraps and cast-offs mostly, but she cherished them. The scientists at Artistos, Fremont's one city, would have used tablets to record data, which was all well and good, but her grandpa had taught her the joy of documenting specimens with careful strokes on paper she held in her own hands. Besides, she never would have been able to sneak off with the tech unnoticed.

Sliding from her cot to the floor with utmost care, she held her breath lest she draw the next one sharp and loud and disturb those she wished to leave sleeping. As she crept from the wagon she trembled, still awed by the uncommon ease with which she now moved.

She had been born with legs twisted and barely controlled, muscles and tendons drawn too short and tight. At Artistos, the colony doctors had corrected them the best they could, but certain things had been beyond them by the time she had been born. While she had grown able to walk, her gait proved awkward and rolling, not to mention painful.

Now, thanks to *them*—the *altered* that came to Fremont less than a year ago claiming the planet as their own, supposedly all legal and binding and not meaning squat, or so her Papa said— Sala's legs were as straight and smooth and able to move as if they'd never been twisted up, even if it had taken her six months to learn how to use them proper. Long, long months, but nothing compared to the almost twelve years she'd spent hobbled, watching others move freely, playing and exploring, *discovering* new things while she stayed at camp helping to catalog those things she longed to see first-hand.

Now...*now* she would explore the world she loved for herself. Not in the bits and pieces brought back to camp. Not from the safe conveyance of a wagon or lofted by a harness on her older brother's back as he hiked the wilds. As much as she appreciated Joram's willingness to do that for her, it just wasn't enough to observe. This...this was her chance to *live*...to discover new things first hand. For that alone she reveled in the transformation of her body. And yet it would be a lie to say all was now well for her. Sala had grown used to being stared at with pity, but the looks most other Roamers gave her had begun to change, ranging from uncomfortable to awed to cold and mistrustful.

Sala hardly cared what any of them thought, or so she told herself. There had already been looks before she was changed, so what if there were looks after? Her freedom was worth tolerating the attention, however uncomfortable. Determination firmed her features as she wended her way through the camp with quiet practiced motions, scrunching down small and pausing absolutely still wherever she hid as those ending their watch handed off their duties to those just coming on. Once they settled she resumed her slow, careful trek, keeping to the deep shadows of the wagons or terrain until she reached the brush surrounding the camp.

Excitement tingled across every nerve like the current that built in the air before an electrical storm as she stood at the edge of the hebra pens, murmuring soft, soothing noises to calm them before they betrayed her. Faint tremors went through her and anticipation clenched her belly as she stared out at the brush.

She had never been beyond the camp on her own.

Clutching her pouch, her gaze darted all around her in the faint pre-dawn light. A smile warmed her face and tears pressed against her eyes as she stepped away from the enclosure into the trees mentally cataloging things as she passed them. Pongaberries, just ripe and ready for picking, if only she could climb that high. Twintrees. Redberry bushes—also heavy with fruit. Ferns and sawgrass, creepers and nettles. So many species of plants she had never seen up close, only in sketches or as loose leaves or berries or twigs.

There wasn't much in the way of wildlife about. Likely a good thing, as her movements weren't that swift, but there were plenty of insects, with which she was already familiar. Still...to see them in the wild... Almost, she lost herself as she watched a fire wasp industriously gather tiny globes of dew to take back to its nest. Shaking herself from the wonder of her observation, Sala strove to remember how near she stood by the camp. To stay here was to risk discovery and the end of her first unsupervised excursion.

Continuing on her way through the brush, she headed for the perimeter, inside the sensors—if only just—but enough outside of camp that the landscape and wildlife remained mostly undisturbed. For a while she just wandered, taking care to avoid tripvines and sawgrass as she scanned for any plant or beastie she didn't recognize from her cataloging efforts. Mostly, though, she just enjoyed her new freedom of movement. Not just the ease of taking a step, but doing so without pain or fear she would overbalance and fall. And without others hovering nearby, trying to appear they weren't, just in case she tumbled.

All too soon she grew winded and her legs began to ache. She found a somewhat comfortable spot beneath a twintree and carefully lowered herself to the ground. For a time she just sat there, enjoying the song of Fremont as the night insects wound down to their rest and the birds began to stir and sing their morning song. Sighing with contentment, Sala drank from her flask and nibbled an energy bar, then took out her parchment and pencil nub. With a care and attention to detail learned at Grandpa's side she drew and documented the area surrounding her. Sawgrass and ferns and flowers, mostly, with the occasional insect clinging to a blade of grass. All familiar, common elements that had surrounded her all her life, or recent finds she had helped catalog after someone else's discovery, but she cherished her first opportunity to observe them closely in their natural environ. While she longed to discover something new, for now she contented herself with studying nature and practicing the observation skills she would need when she did find that unique discovery, which she *would* find one day.

Sala focused so completely on her work that she barely realized how bright the morning grew or how long she had been out, until a rustling in the brush nearby startled her. She jerked her head up as her pencil point veered across her drawing, cutting a sharp line over a flower she had been delicately shading. A few yards beyond the perimeter sensors a cluster of ferns swayed where before they had been still. Sala peered closely but could not see what had disturbed them.

The birds around her had fallen silent.

A shiver skated across her shoulders. She remained within the perimeter, but as far as she could be from the encampment— and any help the others could offer. It had been unwise to lose track of herself like this. The morning grew late. If she strained she could make out the sounds of the camp waking. She gathered her things and pushed herself up from where she sat, bracing against the tree. As she hurried back as best she could she heard more rustling behind her and could not help but look behind her, fearing to see a pawcat or demon dog tracking her. She frowned. She saw no sign of those predators, but...but she would almost swear she saw a person disappear into the brush.

Sala did not bother with silence as she returned to camp. Instead she reached into her satchel for the collapsible bowl, stopping beside the redberry bush to harvest the ripe fruit. Surely Mama would not protest the treat, or think to question what else Sala may have been up to so early once she presented it to her.

"Good morning. Look what I brought," she said as she approached her mother, who appeared to be packing.

"Hurry, we're breaking camp. Akashi wants to be out of here within the hour."

Sala didn't dare frown, but her good cheer drained away. This was a settled camp, meant for a prolonged stay. That gave her more range of freedom. If they resumed roaming she would have a better chance at finding something new, but less likelihood of being able to sneak away to do so. She couldn't help it. Her lips turned down and her breath hitched just a little. Mother looked up sharply but said nothing.

"Come, Sala," she heard Papa call from the door of their wagon. "Eat this, then go help the catalogers secure the specimens."

His expression tightened as she drew near, his eyes shadowed, but then he smiled as she reached him and tousled her hair. Her papa loved her, but he was not happy it had taken the *altered* to help her. Only Mama's pleading and a long conversation with Akashi convinced him it was the only choice. Still, there were times he seemed guarded, as if he suspected more than her legs had been changed.

That was silly. Wasn't it? She would know. Wouldn't she?

Not liking those thoughts, Sala smiled an anxious smile up at Papa and hugged herself close to him. She didn't relax until his arms came around her and hugged back. The moment was fleeting, though. After just a few seconds he patted her shoulder and gently pushed her away.

"Here, now. We don't have much time."

Sala nodded and took the nutrient bar from him. She obediently nibbled at the edges. It sat heavy in her gut, along with the one she'd eaten earlier, as she headed for the research wagon.

No one told Sala the reason they had left their camp. Ultimately, they didn't have to. Even among the Roamers, idle gossip was a thing, and what tongue wouldn't waggle over the rumor of *altered* prowling around the wilds? The little Sala overheard made no sense. The kindest merely called the newcomers unnatural; those who spoke with more anger swore they were monsters and that they meant the settlers harm. More than one claimed they intended to steal the planet. That made no sense to Sala. How did one steal a planet? Fremont had more than enough room for them all. Besides, the altered had been kind to her and made her better. Why do that if they only meant to hurt everyone?

And yet, Sala felt doubt darken her thoughts. She could tell her parents worried, and even Akashi—the most calm and accepting of anyone she knew—had ordered them to break camp. Reportedly, the guards had found tracks just outside the perimeter. Human tracks, or mostly.

Sala thought of the rustling she'd heard in the underbrush the day they had broken camp and shivered.

"Everything okay, sweetie?"

She looked up at her mother, her eyes wide, certain worry bled through her expression.

"Sala?"

"Sorry, Mama. I was just...do you think they're following us?" She said 'us', but she thought 'me'.

Mama frowned and her gaze darted toward the edges of their current camp, where Fremont's wild loomed, more than sufficient to hide both man and beast. "Don't be silly. Why would they?"

Sala had no answer for her. She didn't know. But even if she had, what could she say that wouldn't sound preposterous?

She rested her head against her mother briefly, then went back to sketching the latest batch of specimens, new variations of old finds. The subtle differences both fascinated and frustrated her. Oh, how she wanted to discover something new...

The next morning the Roamers resumed roaming. Sala sat beside her father on the driver's bench of their wagon and tried not to think about the *altered*. Instead she watched the hebras straining to pull the wagons up the tail end of the Eastern Trail, breaking off to follow what Sala called the Crooked Back Path, for the bumpy way it followed the edge of the mountain. She pictured it like the spine of a giant lying on his side and told herself tales about his long journey as she clutched tight to the bench in an effort to stay put. The hebras found this route difficult and even the camp dogs struggled to keep up, but Mama explained the need to break their routine in case they *were* being followed. And so they continued for about a week until they reached a new camp between the river and the cliffs, one they had not used before, having only discovered it at the end of the last season on their way back to Artistos.

Sala twitched with excitement as they drew up to the not-quite cavern. She could picture the nearby river overflowing its bounds each rainy season for millennia, rolling and raging against the cliff that towered over it, never managing more than to carve away at its toes. Or so she imagined.

Whatever the cause, something had worn away the cliff face until it formed a deep, scooped-out pocket, the opening twelve feet high at the mouth and angling down toward the back until even Sala could reach up and touch the worn rock without stretching. All the wagons nestled nicely, if a bit closely, in the space, which offered protection on all but one facing. At the back a proper cave, small and dark, led deep into the cliff. The children—particularly Sala—were forbidden to explore it, but she knew some of the others already had.

Let them. She couldn't care less about a dank, dark hole.

She turned and faced the thriving wilderness, her gaze intent. The plants and bugs and beasties…They waited for her, along with all manner of opportunities to find something new and wondrous. Her eager grin twisted into a grimace. All of it out there…and there was next to no hope of her exploring. The tension had only grown as signs of trespass had been discovered *within* the perimeter sensors at the last nightly camp, with no alarm sounded. The guards continued to amplify security, to say the least.

Sala jumped as a hand came to rest on her shoulder, her thoughts still firmly on intruders.

"Whoa…"

Her muscles loosened as she looked up at Joram. He was ten years older than her and towered overhead as much as Papa did, if not more. Of course, she was tiny—just over four feet tall, thanks to how she had been born—so even those her own age stood over her, when they bothered to be near her at all.

As if privy to her thoughts, Joram knelt down. His arm settled around her waist. She leaned into his comforting presence. "I have to go report in," he said softly, "but we could go exploring after…"

Oh how Sala wanted to say yes, but Joram was a scout. She knew reporting would not be quick. She turned her head to look at him. Weariness had etched faint creases around his eyes and drew down on the corners of his mouth, despite his ready smile. How she loved her brother, more inclined than anyone else in her life to figure out how to make her wishes happen rather than point out why they weren't possible. He never dwelled on her differences, had never counted them against her, not even out of concern, like their parents had in their efforts to protect her. For that reason she would not impose on him now. She leaned her forehead against his. Playfully, she wrinkled her nose. "Maybe a swim would be better...you're kind of stinky."

Her brother retaliated with tickles until their laughter echoed through the camp.

The draw to explore, however, proved too much for Sala to resist once Joram put the idea in her head. It had been impossible of late to sneak off pre-dawn, as she had been. But what if she had permission to search in the daylight? When her brother went off to report, Sala gave in to temptation and headed for the far side of the camp, where Mama helped catalog. With the outward semblance of patience, she waited for her mother to acknowledge her.

Her mother finished the entry she was working on before looking up. "Yes, Sala?"

With only a moment's hesitation, Sala ducked her head, then spoke, "Jory is back in camp. May I go exploring?"

Guilt fluttered in her belly. She had not lied with her words, but her mother would assume her brother would be accompanying her. She held still against the impulse to fidget as she waited.

Mama nodded. "Don't be long, though. You're to help prepare for dinner tonight."

"Yes'm," Sala called back, already heading for her treasured supplies, as eager to avoid any questions as she was to explore. She would return well before time to get ready for the evening meal. She had to be back before Akashi cut Joram loose...

With her pouch clutched in hand, she made her way past the wagons to the edge of camp. She glared as several of the other Roamer girls went by, tittering at her progress. Her steps grew increasingly awkward the more she hurried. Let them laugh; she couldn't afford to slow down. What she truly wanted was to run, but the skill was beyond her still-developing coordination. She finally reached the underbrush, glad of the gentle breeze to cool her. Probing through the flora, she discovered a small game trail, likely worn by djuri. Anyone else would have struggled through, but for once Sala was glad of her small stature. The path was perfect for her. Her gaze scoured the brush surrounding the trail, noting the familiar before swiftly moving on. Occasionally, she saw an unusual variant on a specimen she had catalogued before, but she wasn't here to find mutations or subphyla. Nothing short of a new discovery would satisfy her. Something of value. Something of sufficient note to outweigh her transgression, at the very least...

Sala didn't venture far at first. The sounds of camp remained a steady murmur in the background. Briefly, she stopped to sketch an unusual track, but with no other sign of what may have made it she moved on. Soon she got caught up in the hunt for *her* discovery, peering under rocks and bushes, stirring up the dirt. At one point she tried to climb up the trunk of an umbrella tree in pursuit of an insect she was certain she had never seen, even as a specimen or sketch, only to slide down and bark her shin, left ground-bound to watch as the insect disappeared into the foliage. And still she persisted until the murmur of the camp became a whisper. And then a memory, all but forgotten.

The fading light betrayed her, bringing Sala back from the tight focus of her hunt. As she finally noticed the onset of twilight her belly turned, fear and hunger warring in her gut. Distant birdsong filled her ears, nothing more. Whatever trail she'd followed had petered out. Her legs ached and every patch of bare skin bore at least one itching bite or burning scratch. She shivered and clutched the strap of her pouch. She turned in a slow, stumbling circle trying to see some sign of a path, or at the very least a break in the foliage showing the way she had come. But the gentle breeze had grown more forceful erasing any sign of her passage.

Sala could not silence her first whimper, but she ruthlessly strangled the rest. Though she desperately wanted to call out she knew she must not. Pawcats and demon dogs were drawn by sounds of distress. So were other predators. Maybe ones they didn't even know about yet. That she wouldn't know how to defend herself from. Becoming something's dinner was *not* how she wanted to make her new discovery.

Drawing a deep breath, she straightened her spine and calmed herself. If she hadn't been missed already, she would be soon. Someone would come looking for her. Yes, she had been foolish, but Joram had taught her how to survive as no one else had thought to. He believed in her. She would not disappoint him. The two things he taught her as most important were defense and shelter. *If we get separated arm yourself, then find a place you will be safe and stay there,* he'd said every time they'd gone exploring. *Let me come to you. I* will *find you.*

With the memory of his words firmly in her thoughts, she returned to searching the ground, this time for a long, stout branch, something she could use for both support and defense. As she searched she also looked for any source of shelter...an outcrop of rocks, the high roots of a glúin tree, a cave or overhang, anything she could put her back against. The best she could find was a stout twintree. If not for her small size it would have provided no shelter at all. If she could have climbed the tree, she would have, but that remained beyond her skill. As the sky grew darker, she huddled at the base of the trunks, her back pressed against the smooth bark.

In her pouch she had several nutrition bars and water still half-filled her flask, but fear gripped her tight at both belly and throat. The thought of eating or drinking made her feel sick. While the light remained, she watched the surrounding wilderness for movement, her ears straining for any sound that might be danger or deliverance. *Please, Joram,* Sala thought, *please find me soon.*

She struggled not to cry.

Sala woke to a pair of glowing eyes staring out of the darkness.

She shrieked and fumbled for her stick. The eyes crouched lower, as if to pounce. They were joined by a second set. A low, barely heard rumbling came to her ears. By the height and the sound, Sala knew two juvenile pawcats stalked her. The twintree trunks pressed hard against her back as she tried to push herself to her feet. Her long trek and the chill from the ground had tightened her muscles, though, and she ended up tumbling back down. The glowing eyes leapt.

"Joram!" she cried out.

Seemingly out of nowhere—but more likely from the brush behind her—someone snatched Sala's branch from her hands. It wasn't her brother. In the dark, Sala could not make out who it was, but she would have known Joram in utter darkness, let alone starlight. This person stood shorter, slighter, but not by much. Sala's gaze followed the swing of the branch. With precision and force it connected with the leaping predator. She heard a thud, followed by the muffled crack of breaking bones. The creature's cry cut short, followed by brief thrashing that faltered, then stopped all together. Sala's savior raised the branch again, but the shadowy hulk of the second predator already skulked away, its grumbling whine fading with the growing distance.

The predators dealt with, the stranger turned. Something in those movements reminded Sala very much of the pawcat before it lay broken on the ground. The motions were fluid and powerful, dangerous and completely unfamiliar. Swallowing a whimper, Sala shrank back against the tree, her arms hugged around herself more for comfort than any sort of protection.

The form before her went still, then slowly crouched down where it stood, lowering to the ground until its legs were crossed and its hands laid down where a person's knees would be.

"It's okay, little one." The voice belonged to a woman. The words did nothing to reassure. Sala knew all the Roamers, from both bands; the woman was not one of them. She could have been from Artistos, but none of *them* would venture past their barrier, let along this far into Fremont's wilds.

The woman could only be one of the *altereds.*

Sala shrank more into herself, pressed harder into the tree, remembering the recent murmurings about camp. Silently, she begged Joram...or *someone* she knew to hurry.

There was a *click* and a soft, warm glow lit the woman's face.

Drawing a sharp breath, Sala straightened.

If anyone had asked her if she'd memories of the *altered* who fixed her, Sala would have said no, with full confidence. Until this moment, that would have been true, but those eyes...those electric green eyes staring back at her... Startling, but kind. Reassuring, and not for the first time. Sala found it did not matter to her that they were not natural in color.

"Why do you follow us?"

The eyes slowly blinked. The woman remained silent, her expression considering, the way Akashi looked when he carefully chose what words to say.

"To make sure you are well," the *altered* answered in a soft, calm tone. "To make sure what we have done still functions properly for you."

"How do you follow me?" Sala asked, now certain her earlier worry was founded.

The woman blinked again, only faster, as if Sala had startled her, then her eyes lowered slightly. "I am a Wind Reader...one engineered to read the data streams. The tech in your blood, that which repaired you, it speaks to me."

Sala thought on that, not certain how she felt about their 'tech' still being inside her. Surely Papa did not know. He would have been angry. Much more than angry. She prayed he never found out. She couldn't bear if his look toward her changed any more.

"Does that..." Sala's voice broke. "Does that make me... *altered*?"

Compassion softened the woman's eyes, but hurt shadowed them. "No, little one. No. Still your worries. We only repaired you, like setting a broken bone, or removing a tumor. We did not change you as we have been changed."

Sala did not know what to say. Or to believe. There was so much she didn't understand. And so many questions she wanted to ask... Before she could decide on the next, distant cries drew her attention away from the woman, her brother's voice among them.

Joram! He came, as he promised!

Even as joy and relief bubbled up from her heart, Sala's muscles knotted with worry. Not for herself, but for her rescuer. She was startled to discover she no longer feared the *altered* sitting before her. While Sala did not know the woman's name, she remembered her. Knew at some point the woman had comforted her and cared for her when they had remade her body. When she ventured out this day, she had not realized her new discovery would be a rediscovery. A faint recollection surfaced from the time of her surgery, something the woman had once said, which Sala's heart had held to fiercely, if not her memory. *Different is just different, not wrong.* Words that applied as much to Sala herself as to the *altered.*

Again, Sala heard her name called out, distracting her.

Her expression now wary, the woman rose with an ease Sala envied. Without another word, the *altered* stooped and picked up the carcass she had made.

"Wait," Sala called to her, almost whispering, though clearly the searchers were not close enough to hear her. The woman paused, turning to meet her gaze.

"Why...why did you come here?"

"To live free...without conflict."

Sala was old enough to recognize the wry twist to the woman's lips, but not old enough yet to know how to respond.

The woman gave Sala a sad smile, then she turned and left, parting the brush as if it were tissue, the pawcat casually draped over her shoulder. Her departure left no sign and made no sound as Joram's cries drew closer.

It was as if the woman had never been there. It was as if she never would be again.

In seemingly an instant, Sala grew up, and with sadness, she murmured, "I'm sorry."

For whatever little difference it made, in her heart, Sala knew the woman heard her.

This is a story fragment that we found during our first trip to Artistos. It is told by Mayah, Akashi's wife, and is from long before the story told in The Silver Ship and the Sea started. Unlike many of the tales we've found there, this may not have been polished by years of storytelling. At least, it is far more personal than most of the community stories. There is another version of this, which may be the one that entered the mythos of the West Band. In that story, Akashi is not conflicted....

Archival
Story Fragment #1

Brenda Cooper

Stream created August 30th, 230

The child was no more than three. I watched him, looking for differences between him and us.

I sat on the end of a log, with Akashi standing beside me. The child, Liam, stood solemnly by the communal fire, a few feet between him and any of us. It was the band's first night out of Artistos, and we had pulled hard all day up the High Road. Sweat ran in small rivulets down the boy's bronze skin, and still he held his palms out to the fire as if he needed its heat.

I wanted to warm him in my lap even though a week ago we had tried to kill him and all of his kind. We had almost succeeded. He and five others lived.

Some of the band hated him. As if children between two and six could form up as an army and send killing machines at us. As if this babe would develop wings and fly from camp, or extra arms, or flex his fingers and produce knives that have been hidden under his skin.

We had faced all of those things from his kind. A third of our number had died. We had not known peace for so long I couldn't remember it, and I didn't yet smell it in the stances or conversations of the band.

His eyes were deep blue, and the reflected fire in them looked like the sun rising through the sky in early morning. If I saw a difference between him and us it was simply beauty. His limbs had all the right proportions. His arms and legs were unmarred by scratches or bruises or old scars from thorns. His muscles were more defined than any of our children's at three, perhaps more than any of ours at any age. Even though he had been in hiding, and must have been hungry, the only thing that showed deprivation was the way he kept his palms open and close to the fire, growing red with the heat.

He did not show his pain, but he must feel it.

I curled my arm around my mate's leg, noticing how tightly his calf muscles bunched, the way his weight was planted on the ground as if it he forced himself not to move. Akashi also watched the boy, his head slightly cocked so I knew he was evaluating the risks that came with this child.

I glanced again at the silent, stoic boy. "Sweetheart?" I whispered to Aksahi.

"Yes."

"Therese and Steven took in two of them."

I did not have to tell him the subtext. That we led the band and we should take the child. The others had gone to leaders. Therese and Steven led us all. A girl-child had gone to Paloma, who healed us all.

We should take this child.

But Akashi just stared at Liam, his jaw tight, and I didn't whisper anything else. Something had turned inside me as the boy stood, and I didn't want anyone else to take him. In fact, I might fight anyone else who tried. Yet if I pushed Akashi to tell me no, I would not be able to change his mind. I was not—then— a co-leader in the way that Therese was, or a true leader like Nava, later. I was simply Akashi's bride. Like Paloma, I had so far proved barren. That happened to many of us, maybe one or two in ten, and I wanted to hold this perfect boy.

Around the fire, I saw at least two of the other childless women looking at the boy with bare curiosity.

I glared at them.

I rose and took his hand and led him to a sleeping tent. For now, he had been assigned to sleep with Old Margaret, since she lived alone in a large wagon. Two of the men had helped her fashion a small cage for him, so that he would be safe. He had slept there two nights already, and no harm had come to or from him.

When Margaret took him from me, she shook her head and muttered. "No good can come of this."

"Of course it can," I replied.

"He brings back too many memories," she said. "Memories that hurt."

"They will fade."

"Never," she hissed, and took the silent child in with her, presumably to shut him in his cage for the night.

I went back deep in contemplation, hoping for a private conversation with Akashi. But by the time I returned, he was already talking with three of his Council, plotting our route into the mountains. I listened quietly. When Akashi and I married, I became an automatic member of the Council, but that night I had nothing to add, and my thoughts drifted over and over to Liam, and what it must feel like to sleep in a cage.

The moon Destiny had risen in the sky and hung bright overhead by the time Akashi took my hand and led me to the wagon. Even then, he did not want to talk. As soon as we went inside, he folded me in his arms and began to knead the stiff muscles of my back with his fingers. We had not made love since before the last battle, and it felt good and strange to be so close to him, to smell the smoke of the fire and his sweat. I leaned into him, moaning, but my back stayed stiff. Even though he felt like love, I stepped away and turned to face him. "We should take that child," I said.

He stiffened immediately. "We will have one of our own someday."

"You are choosing not to understand."

"I can't do this." He turned away from me and reached up into one of the cupboards above our head and took down a skin of water, pouring a cup and staring out of our small window, even though there was nothing to see but darkness.

"Someone needs to tame him, make him one of us."

"I cannot forgive them yet."

He meant the altered beings who flew down and demanded our land, and then killed so many of us. His own father had been skewered by a man with a sword for a hand. The child's people had been liars. They had been bringers-of-pain-and-weapons. I put a hand on Akashi's shoulder and kept my voice low. "If he sleeps in a cage long enough, he may become an animal."

The muscles under my hand rippled, like those of a dog trying to cast off a flea.

I let my hand fall and turned away.

That night, we slept close but not cuddled. Moonlight fell on his face, which looked troubled even in sleep. His chest rose and fell with his breath, and he muttered unintelligible things from time to time. For the first time since our marriage, I wondered if I could obey him.

Before dawn, I woke to hear a small cry come from the direction of Maggie's wagon. I knew immediately that it was something to do with the boy, and went out still in my nightclothes to hear her telling Khani that when she woke, the cage was empty. I peered into the wagon to see that the bars had been shattered, two of the stout wooden sticks snapped in half.

None of us could have opened the cage that way. Not from inside, not with so little room for leverage.

Liam had revealed one of the differences between him and us.

Strong or not, he was still three, and couldn't possibly hide from us for long. I raced back to our wagon and dressed, alerting Akashi, who cursed (he never cursed) and thus we were the first to follow his trail.

It turns out he was not only strong but fast. He had taken the main path back down to the High Road, perhaps hoping to find the other children. Even though Akashi and I are two of the fastest members of the West Band, it took us a long time to find him. We might have had to go all the way to Artistos if he hadn't fallen and sprained an ankle. He sat in the middle of the path, clutching a rock in his tiny fist, staring at the forest. A demon dog bayed, and then another, the pack going away from us now that we had arrived.

Akashi stopped and stared at Liam.

Another few moments and he would surely have been dead. The look on my beloved's face assured me that Akashi wished we had been slower. I could not hate Akashi for that, but I could not hate Liam for existing.

I left my husband's side and went to the boy. We did not share a language, but he let me pluck the rock from his hand and pick him up. Akashi looked at me. "This is the price for you?" he asked.

"This is for the band," I said.

He stared at me, and at the boy, for a long time. And then he smiled and said only, "I chose the right woman."

And then the other members of the band started to catch up with us. I kept the boy in my arms as we walked back up the road, and the others followed, surrounding us, but giving some distance as well.

There would be work to do.

From David Lee's Journal, undated. Historians believe it may have been from before he ever reached Fremont. It may help illuminate the mental instability of powerful Wind Readers.

Blood Song

Brenda Cooper

Ship's engines beat my blood
data is a ghost
Is living
Is a ghost
Is living
Is a ghost, living

The ship and I kiss,
each of our air pulled
through membranes
through lungs.
I am the ship
is in
that air.
We breathe each other.

To recall my body requires the dig of fingernail
into flesh, the hollow of a parched and empty
body. It hurts to be only one.

This is a scrap of story that was found in the archives on Fremont during the research trip that Sister Mary Martin Moss commissioned even before she started the Academy. Because it was found then—and on Fremont, which has no sophisticated nets or Wind Readers of its own—it is deemed to be authentic without the detailed vetting that occurs for other stories. The roamers on Fremont were partly an oral society: they told each other stories. This is a first-person journal entry from the viewpoint of Sasha, the girl with the white streak in her hair who Joseph eventually named his companion dog after. It is highly polished, so we think this version came after it was told and re-told around campfires under the many moons of Fremont.

Archival
Story Fragment #2

Brenda Cooper

It was the summer migration, and we were fat with the bounty of our three days in town. Many of the wagons pulled new yearling animals behind them, goats and hebras and dogs just barely trained.

The cool morning breeze smelled of spring flowers. I sat alone on Chelo's wagon-seat, minding my own business, which was being watchful. Even though the dust and noise of our passage had surely scared game and predator alike away, I watched the trees along edges of the road for djuri sign or the yellow eyes of paw-cats. That is what we did, we roamers. We watched.

My parents were near the back, and one of the nicest things about that morning was being able to ride by myself with no well-meant lectures from Mom or teases from the twins, Kyre and Loma. Chelo's wagon rolled near the middle of a long line, rocking its way ever-so-slowly up the High Road behind Stripes. The hebra made it look like work, even though I knew it really wasn't. Stripes stood tall for a hebra, her head taller than the top of the wagon. She was generally well-mannered, if a bit vain. She kept her head up and pulled the hard way, as if still insisting she was too good to be harnessed. Or maybe she was just too proud to dig in like the other beasts, head down, haunches straining. She, too, watched. Always.

We had already made it to the part of the High Road where the cliff is more a steep hill, a jumble of rocks. They were dangerous. Chelo and Joseph's parent's died in a rockfall near here, and a few boulders looked like they might fall on us at any moment even without an earthquake. Some appeared to be balanced so lightly that a summer breeze might send them down to crack our fragile wooden wagons open like bird's eggs.

Indeed, when Chelo and Liam scrambled up the steep hill an hour earlier, rocks the size of small dogs had bounced down into the road and startled one of the young hebras being walked beside the wagon behind me. Chelo and Liam made the ascent look easy, the high tinkle of their laughter the last real sign I had of them. If I'd been climbing that, I would have been too winded to laugh. Of course, they were not tired, and sounded like they always did, happy and strong and in love.

I didn't expect any sign of them until dusk. They did this every year, a ritual they shared with me since they needed a wagon driver and Chelo had no family. That year, I was still so young I thought they were simply sneaking off to make love in some private place.

If Chelo weren't my best friend, I'd have been terribly jealous. Chelo was everyone's friend, of course, but I was the one she'd picked to drive her wagon and keep her hebra. Mom had tried, as usual, to keep me from it, but Dad had reminder her rather gruffly that I would be old enough for my own wagon in two years and so the practice would do me good. They had glared at each other for a long moment, then kissed, and they hadn't even insisted I make sure the wagon was near theirs.

It felt good to be so adult. I didn't want to screw up.

Everything seemed fine until Stripes turned her head all the way around stared down at me. Her eyelashes and beard stood out like silhouettes as the sun haloed her head, and I couldn't quite make out the look in her eyes.

"She'll be back later," I reassured her.

Stripes tossed her head, still walking forward while looking backward. Her tack jingled as buckles scraped against each other.

I had taught her how dangerous that was myself, forcing a fall. I snapped at her. "Pay attention!"

She turned her head back around, her displeasure evident in the way she kept her long neck stiff and shook it from time to time, as if a swarm of flies had settled on her skin.

Stripes had a reputation for being as stubborn as her master. She started prancing. She'd never misbehaved like this for me—

I had helped break her to harness and shown Chelo how to rub her down and feed her and watch for sores and thorns. I shifted my weight and gathered the reins closer in my hands, holding them just tight enough to signal that I was in control.

Akashi rode by, glancing at Stripes, who continued prancing. He pulled up his own mount and narrowed his eyes at the fractious hebra before looking at me in that way of his, all intensity focused entirely on me. Although we were lucky to have him in the West Band, I still didn't like being under his regard. "Can you handle her?" he asked.

He himself had helped train me to train hebras, so his words stung. "Of course I can."

A trace of doubt touched his eyes. Maybe he was like Stripes, worried about Chelo and Liam. Maybe he knew where they went. But if he did, he didn't pass it on to me. He just nodded and went on riding the line, offering help, encouragement, or admonition as required.

No sooner had he truly gone a few wagons past, when Stripes reared up in her traces. I tugged her down, almost standing myself. I smelled the fear on her then, and her nostrils quivered.

She bugled, a high ululating call that rose up the cliff wall and bounced out into the clear over the valley to our right. Surely even the people in Artistos, far below, heard her. And if they didn't hear her, they heard the others, as first Brown Bead and then Girl-of-Grass and then Nix and Star and Moon-face and eventually all hundred or more hebras bugled together, as if they were all watching and all of them had spotted a pack of predators.

I tensed, hoping they wouldn't run.

Dogs began to bark.

A high-pitched whine touched my ears even over the calls and stamping feet of the frightened animals. Stripes had stopped in her traces, feet planted and splayed, looking up.

So I looked up.

A silver cylinder floated above our heads. It was bigger than our biggest wagon, and smaller than the silver ship Joseph had stolen from the plain. Not quite round, but as if a round thing had been stepped on and squished just a bit. Two flat wedges came out the sides, like a mash between fins and wings, widest at the back.

It wiggled, as if it were waving.

The noise it made grew until it was louder than the hebras and the dogs, until it stilled them all. The cylinder seemed to hold in the air, to float for just long enough that I was scared it would fall down into the void below and land on the town or in the Lace River.

But then it—simply left. It moved so fast that it became quickly small and quiet, a silver bee going away from us over the ocean and then nothing.

In its aftermath a silence fell. No barks. No bugles. Just the whisper of breeze in the trees. Everywhere I looked the drivers and walkers and handlers looked at the empty sky.

A child cried.

People began to call to their dogs and to settle the hebras.

Stripes let out a long low moan, a sound I'd never heard from a hebra before. I immediately knew what she was telling me. Chelo and Liam had gone. There had been no sign they meant to leave. Surely if they had known, Chelo would have spent an extra moment with me, or given Stripes an extra treat.

She hadn't even taken her clothes.

Akashi rode up and down the line, calling orders to move, to keep going, to gather, to focus. The inside of my chest felt cold and empty. Stripes walked ahead of me with her head bowed.

After a hundred steps and a hundred more, I noticed the warmth of the day. Sweat fell down my face, mixing with tears on my cheek, and I looked up at the sky over and over.

It remained empty.

Once, when Akashi rode by, I swear I saw tears on his face, too.

Liam was his son, and Chelo my friend.

The next time he came by, the tears were gone, but they had left faint tracks in the road-dust that coated his cheeks. He couldn't take my hand while we were moving, but he held his out in a gesture of support and his voice rose over the sound of the turning wagon wheels and the breath of dogs and the clop of hebras hooves on the hard road. "I knew about the skimmer. It's called the *Burning Void*. It isn't ours."

Of course it wasn't. The invaders had brought it, and that was where Chelo and Joseph went—to wherever their first parents' left things like *the Burning Void*. To a secret place. "Do you know where they went or why they left?"

He shook his head. "They can't fly it."

I looked up at the sky, light blue so the middle above me was almost white. I knew who it had to be, although she was only a face and a set of rumors to me. "Kayleen?"

"Only she or Joseph could fly it."

Joseph had flown away seasons ago, and never returned. Far away. Off the planet. Fear seized my stomach. "Can the skimmer go to the stars?"

"It must be too small."

"Do you think they'll come back?"

He swallowed, looking both angry and lost at once, like the two emotions warred in him. He almost never looked that vulnerable, not to me. "I hope they do."

"I will hope with you."

In that moment, Stripes snorted and looked up at both of us, as if she understood. Perhaps she did. Hebras understood it when we gave them commands, after all.

Akashi rode on up the line, his head bowed.

I wished Chelo and Liam were back and that Mom was lecturing me about staying in her sight when we got above the High Road.

At that moment, I had no idea how much would change before I saw them again. I only knew that the place on the bench where Chelo often sat beside me felt cold and empty.

The Street of All Designs

Brenda Cooper

Jenna sent me and Alicia to Li City to look for mods. I hoped something would distract her from her fascination with flying.

I should have known better.

"I want wings." She squinted as she stared up at Tiala's gold-and-red bird, Bell. Bell was a living thing, light and fast, with metal parts and the voice of an angel. At the moment she was silent, except the silk of her wings through the air. As Bell flew between silvery buildings, sunlight painted diamonds and stars on her feathers, so bright she was hard to look at but easy to follow.

Tiala probably watched us through the many cameras on the bird, but I tried to ignore that.

Bell was only one wonder among millions on Silver's Home. Even though we'd been on the planet a few months now, the press of people and the constant hum of conversation assaulted me from all sides.

Alicia repeated, "I want wings."

She didn't want wings like Bell's. She wanted wings big enough to carry her above her broken soul. "Why do you want to lose your ability to run? I'd be happy with a bird like Bell. Something to follow me around, let me put a camera on its neck so I can see anything I need to."

"I'd rather fly than run."

"That's not nearly as useful." But Alicia seldom listened to anyone. I'd worked all week to get her alone so I could convince her to choose a mod that would help us save our people in the war, and all she could say was she wanted to fly. I leaned down and whispered in her ear. "I'm happy enough to be a strongman, and you should be happy enough to be a pretty girl."

She smiled, standing on tiptoe and looking around. "You sound old, Bryan. Jenna said we could pick any mod. I want wings."

If I didn't know she was designed to be our risk taker, I would have been shocked to see her so happy in this strange place that made me nervous. She dressed in almost nothing herself. Just a sleeveless blue shirt that barely covered her top and behind, and the shortest blue shorts under it I'd ever seen. I didn't like that. It would not have been allowed on Fremont, and perhaps I was more a creature of that place than I wanted to be.

Alicia's crystal data necklace glittered when we walked under lights, another sign of how much she'd taken to Silver's Home.

"Jenna said wings take too long." I searched the crowd for a flier, hoping to remind her how pained they looked on the ground. But we were nowhere near a flyspace, and there were only walking people on this street—tall ones, wide ones like me, women who'd chosen mods to make them desirable and showed them off by wearing almost nothing. "Besides, you wouldn't fit in a spaceship with wings."

"He's right." A woman's voice from two inches behind my right ear. I startled and turned, tense and ready to defend Alicia. She looked about our age—maybe twenty or so—but here I bet she was two hundred. She had blonde hair and blue eyes as astonishing in color as Alicia's violet ones, and she smelled like the grass plains from home in spring, when they were a sea of yellow and white flowers. She smiled at us—coy and innocent, even her eyes—before she stuck out her hand. "I'm Induan."

"I'm Bryan." I ignored her hand. "How'd you get there?"

She grinned and turned to Alicia. "Jenna sent me to look for you."

"Figures." Alicia glowered at her, and she, too ignored the outstretched hand. "Why not be a flier?"

Induan hesitated, and I imagined she was trying to find a way to answer Alicia's question with something other than contempt for a failure to see the obvious.

Induan drew her pale hand back, and I felt a slight pang of regret that we were being so rude. She told Alicia, "Being a flier's even harder than being a swimmer. Jenna suggested I try and keep you two out of trouble."

I stiffened. Keeping Alicia safe was my job. It was hard work in this strange place full of hidden lies and hidden knives and beautiful women who appeared from thin air, but I loved my role. "How'd you sneak up on us?"

"I'm quiet."

So she wasn't going to tell me. "What does Jenna want?"

"She wants you to figure out what you want to become. You leave in a week."

What I wanted to become? *What I wanted to become?* You couldn't choose that at home. What you wanted to be inside, or what you wanted to learn. But you couldn't change your body. But here? It was one of the secrets of this world, and it struck me silent.

On the first day after Joseph landed the silver ship *New Making,* Jenna told us these people changed rivers and islands. I had not taken the claim literally, but the words of this girl-woman made me re-evaluate Jenna's statement.

Induan cocked her head at me, like the camp dogs used to, and wrinkled her brow.

I felt slow, but I finally forced a few words out. "Thanks. For finding us. I guess."

Alicia glared at her, but at least she didn't pop out with the word *wings.* Instead, she said, "How do we know what's possible?"

Induan's grin looked impish and full of secrets. She threaded through the sparse crowd. Bell followed the girl, banking tight golden circles above her head. Alicia and I glanced at each other, and then followed, Alicia practically skipping.

My attention kept snagging on new colors of hair and new shapes for eyes. Some people ignored me, some smiled, some looked wary. Many were lost inside their heads, walking around obstacles well enough, but gone into the data like a lover's embrace. Wind Readers.

Here, on their home turf, the people of Silver's Home appeared to be a race of distracted beauty.

What would they be like if we fought them? What weapons were they carrying that I couldn't see? If Marcus's warning was correct, when we got back home we might have to fight people with magic made of nanotech and flesh, the way the bird Bell was both.

And all I had now was flesh, stronger and faster than anyone on Fremont, but weaker than many people here. Maybe weaker than all of them.

At home, I'd been the strongest person on the planet.

Induan turned a corner around a tall grey-and-smoke colored building. I started wondering what kind of weapons she had, or what she could change into with a push of a button. And then I turned the corner and forgot to worry about her, since my mouth gaped open and my feet stopped so suddenly that a tall thin man with a six-legged cat on his shoulder bumped into me. "Sorry," he mumbled, and flowed around me, the cat's ringed tail twitching.

A smoke-colored arch hung between buildings, ten man-heights or so tall. Below it, translucent figures of humans, or parts of humans sometimes, floated in the air. They had extra muscles in their backs, webbed feet, knives for fingernails, hairy pelts like on an animal, and more. And—of course—there were wings. Although not, I thought, as beautiful as the one Alicia wanted. These were more like contraptions. Mechanical rather than flesh.

A faint smell like burned twintree fruit bothered me. The air felt damp and tingly under the signs, the way it feels just before rain.

"Welcome..." Induan twirled her hand in a small flourish and Bell rose higher as if in response, flying right through a sign for a shop that apparently sold extra arms. "...to the Street of All Designs."

"How do they do that?" Alicia asked.

"Which one?"

"Making all the pictures in the air."

"Oh." Induan wrinkled her nose. "There's water and the barest bit of power and...I don't remember. Some other elements they put into the microclimate here that lets them show the im-ages in three dimensions." She blew on the bottom of a foot hanging just above her head, and the image shimmered and winked, then stabilized. "There's other places like this, but visible ads are banned on the main streets."

The man with the cat was already halfway down the street, just walking, apparently immune to the strange forms bobbing above him. "There are other places to get mods?"

Induan let us look around but kept us moving. "Well, sure. But not nearby. There's always specialty shops. But you don't have permission for beta mods. What do you need to do?"

Keep my family from dying here or back home. "I need to be... strong. And lethal."

"Well, you look strong already. So, shouldn't you choose something that will surprise?" She pointed up. "Like cameras in the back of your head?"

"I don't want to look different."

Alicia laughed. "A camera would help you *see* differently." She grinned. "Or you could just get better eyes."

I shivered and blinked, queasy at the idea of trading a part of me for a different part. "Give me a minute to look around, okay?"

Induan looked at me quizzically. "Can you? Do you have an interface?"

"I can see."

Alicia took Induan's hand. My risk-taker, bonding in moments. "Give him a little time. He'll decide if we don't push him."

So now I felt stupid, and vulnerable. And backward. For the first time in my life I wasn't the oddest being on the planet. I wasn't even close. So why did I want to go back home so badly?

"Come on," Alicia said, "Let's look for me. I'm glad I'm here, even if Bryan isn't."

The shards of glass in her words drove me to turn away from her so she couldn't see how they stung. I'd never turned away from her before, but now she wanted to impress this total stranger.

I paced under the advertisements, staring at each one from as many angles as I could. Every choice looked wrong. I didn't want prehensile toes; my shoes wouldn't fit. Or legs that were obviously much stronger, but so bulky they wouldn't feel right. All the mods that would look right on a strongman like me would make me even bigger, or even stronger, or give me extra arms.

But what would I do with extra arms when I didn't need then to shoot extra weapons I already didn't have?

There wasn't anything I could imagine doing to myself.

I started looking around for Induan and Alicia by checking near the wings, although I knew they were an impossibility. I didn't see them walking through the various weapons displays, which was a different kind of relief. Alicia had big, fast anger in her. Big, fast everything emotional, really, but I didn't want to worry about her with a weapon. They weren't anywhere near the mods designed to make women beautiful, but of course they did not need those things.

I finally spotted a brief flash of light on Bell's wings, and Alicia, standing below her, under moving advertisements for fins and gills. Induan was nowhere to be seen, but Alicia was a vision. She stood poised and curious, like she belonged here. Her bare legs gleamed. I swallowed and walked up to her, waited for her to notice me. When she turned her violet gaze toward me, she looked light and happy. Curious. And a little like she was bursting with something to tell me. But she asked me first. "Did you find one?"

"You can have mine. You can have two, if you want two."

The shape of her face told me she was about to say yes, but them she stopped. "No. You take one. You want to go save us all on Fremont, and if you die because I stole your mod from you, I'll never forgive myself."

"I'm giving it. You're not stealing it."

"Jenna wants us to each get one."

"Since when do you do what she says?"

She stopped dead for a moment, and took in a breath and let it out and took in another one. "This is big. And... what if we never get back?"

"I can't. Everything looks like I wouldn't be myself."

She pursed her lips. "But we're already different. We've always been different."

"That's not the same as wanting to be different from myself."

She leaned over and gave me a quick, hard hug. "It'll be okay. You'll still be yourself."

"How will I know?" I felt pressed toward a future that frightened me more than being beat up by gangs of jealous teenagers back home.

Induan's voice came from right behind me again. "You are always yourself, even if you change."

I twitched and turned. She was close, way too close. She couldn't have just casually walked in. I sounded angry even to my own ears, a shade too loud for this quiet place. "Where did you come from?"

She didn't take a step back. Her voice was quiet as she said, "I've been right here."

I took a step toward her.

I didn't mean her any harm, and I wouldn't have hurt her. But she wasn't there.

Maybe a blur, at best, and then she was gone. I drew in a breath and straightened up. There were a few other people shopping for new parts, no one close. They didn't seem to have noticed Induan popping in and out of the world. But maybe people popped in an out of reality around here all the time. Maybe she was only a little less a hologram than the advertisements all around us. I turned toward Alicia, who had her slender fingers over her mouth and looked like she could barely keep from doubling over with laughter.

Induan had included Alicia in her secret, whatever it was.

All my life, I'd wondered why people could be so cruel, but we had never been cruel to each other. Never. Never been anything but supportive. It felt like being taunted by the original humans back home. No, it didn't. It was worse. I ducked and started walking away, a touch of anger starting to curl up the back of my neck.

I walked out of the Street of All Designs, turned the corner, and found a space with a sky hanging above me instead of humans even stranger than me. The scrap of sky comforted me. The blue was brighter than home, but only a little. It still reminded me of Fremont.

How had it happened that I had come to this place? Even though years had passed, I had slept them away in a cold dreamless drawer in the *New Making.* When I awoke, the same cuts and bruises I'd taken when the Fremont toughs beat me up had been red and purple and real. And then healed, almost like magic, so all I felt now was tightness in my skin where the deepest cuts had been.

I couldn't walk safely while looking up, so I made myself look ahead and walk through strangers until I found a tree in this place of buildings. I leaned against a building, alien like all the rest in size and material, but I kept it at my back and watched the tree and the sky above the tree.

They found me, of course. The building at my back kept Induan from sneaking up, but it didn't keep Bell from circling above my head, trilling. The two women walked side by side, heads bent together and chattering like old friends even though they had just met. They were nearly the same size and shape, although opposite in color, Alicia dark and Induan light. Shadow and light.

Alicia saw me first. Her face softened when she did, and she quickened her step.

The fist of anger gripping my insides lightened a bit at that, and I tried to smile for her.

Before they said anything, they stood right next to each other in front of me, and Alicia said, "Take Induan's hand."

I did. It was warm. Flesh. Even a bit sweaty. I no longer doubted a human stood physically in front of me. She blinked, and smiled, and suddenly looked a bit shy.

Induan took her hand away and Alicia said, "Watch."

Induan smeared for an eyeblink, and then she was gone. The space where she had been was so empty that people walked behind it, and I saw them.

"Squint," the air said, using Induan's voice.

Shaking, I did as she said. It didn't matter.

Then it did.

The first sight I caught of her was a leftover dot of red against the clear sky after a man with a flowing red shirt walked by. It took another breath to notice a smear of green near the ground. "I can't really see her even when I know she's there."

Induan touched me and a piece of my arm disappeared under her hand. I flinched as far into the cold building at my back as I could, and couldn't stop myself from saying, "No, please, no," before I plunged my hand back at her, making myself accept the invisibility and know my arm was still whole. She took my hand, holding it, a force alone as far as the eye could tell.

Then she let go and smeared into visible again.

Alicia never stopped watching me. She had the sense to let me get my breath before she said, "That's the one I picked. Induan is a strategist, and she thinks it's the best one for an unknown situation."

Better than wings? But I didn't dare say it out loud.

"So you can still have one. You don't have to give me yours."

Two pretty girls with the will to become invisible stared at me, patient. But no matter how patient, I had to answer. I had set off this morning to pick a mod. I had been looking for a new weapon, not to become something else. Not to change myself.

I looked past Alicia and Induan, at the tall and thin men and women walking one by one or in groups. They could change themselves. They had. If nothing else, they were all beautiful, even in their strangeness. There was no age here, no infirmity. My eye went to a pair of fliers, the first I'd seen today. They did hobble. But in spite of the pain that shone through the tight lines of their mouths and the careful way they walked, they looked transcendent. Their wings glittered in the light.

Perhaps I needed to find a way to see changing myself as a gift. To see it as becoming. "Maybe you two can help me choose."

Indian and Alicia both nodded, and Induan smiled graciously.

I was going to have to outgrow our backward home to live here. "Thanks."

As we walked back toward The Street of All Designs, I leaned over to Alicia and whispered, "Maybe when we come back you can choose wings."

WATER LILY

HUNTING GROUNDS

BRENDA COOPER

Romi watched the modified paw-cat lean out from the tree branch, almost directly over the Hunter, haunches bunched, contemplating. The Hunter stood small, lean almost to the point of thinness. Unusual here. Romi preferred the obviously augmented, the over-confident. He swallowed as the man stared up at the cat, the two of them locked in gaze and stance, both ready.

The Hunter took a step sideways.

The cat didn't move, except for a slight tremor in her back leg left over from the last hunt. The tremor hadn't been visible this morning, or even later, after the cat had been harried through the trees for hours. A failure on Romi's part; Keepers were supposed to assure the safety of the predators they kept. Whatever his error had been, it could cost the cat her life. She had slowed. Some days, cats could win by wearing out their Hunters, but this Hunter had done the opposite and worn out the cat.

The Hunter raised his right arm straight overhead. Something new.

Romi held his breath, flicked his eye so he saw through the camera view that showed the man's back. Muscles rippled, like two rivers running uphill beside his spine.

Romi willed the cat to move.

The Hunter lowered his arm slowly toward the cat.

The cat's golden eyes didn't stray from the man for even a moment. It sank low, its forequarters below its hips, dug its elongated front claws into the wide branch.

The Hunter's arm slashed air.

The cat pushed away from the branch, fluid, deadly.

Darts flew from the man's fingers, a ghost of a weapon, there because Romi knew they were, not because of anything his eyes or the camera verified. He winced as the man twisted aside, just avoiding the cat's full pounce. Claws raked his arm. Three thick stripes of red welled up before bloodbots could staunch the flow.

To his credit, the Hunter didn't react to the clawing or the blood, he just kept swirling away, low and fast.

The cat landed off-balance, listing a bit to the right. She clung to the floor, wide-eyed, affected by whatever the man had hit her with. Romi ground his teeth and made a mental note to replay the recording later.

The size difference was clear now that the combatants scrambled across the same surface. The cat's shoulders came almost to the man's, its legs as long as his.

The Hunter's right foot slipped out from under him, the first mistake he had made today. Fear flashed across his face, thinning his lips. As he leapt, determination showed in ways Romi hadn't seen before, a decisive change. The end of the hunt was near, the outcome still uncertain. In this moment, the Hunter knew he could lose.

Romi was used to this moment, used to the uncertainty, but still he felt his own muscles bunch and tense.

The Hunter managed to stand again, to leap backward, keeping his eyes on the cat.

The cat slouched toward him, still slower than she should be.

The Hunter held his crouch, something nearly impossible here, something even altered human nerves almost always fought against in the face of an advancing predator.

The cat also crouched, gliding forward with enough control that her victory looked inevitable.

The Hunter leapt, his jump acrobatic, graceful. His legs opened in the air and he scissored, the gymnastics of his move elegant and fast.

The cat leapt away but the man landed on her haunches, grabbed for fur, slid off.

As the Hunter fought to regain his footing, the cat twisted and pounced. Forepaws bore the Hunter to the ground. Claws raked holes in his chest. Blood stained the cat's tawny coat.

The Hunter pulled his head in, rolled small as if he could hide from the six hundred pounds of cat on top of him.

The cat pawed at him, forcing him to uncurl. Her mouth closed on the man's head, her thick neck and heavy shoulders forcing him to stay down. Her jaws clenched.

The Hunter drummed a heel on the floor and arched his back before stilling.

Against his will, against all his training, Romi cheered and pumped his fist in the safety of the empty room. Then he shut his eyes tight and willed his fists to unclench. By the time he was through the door, he had his Keeper's face back on.

He loped fast, the feeling of triumph driving him. He found the cat standing still by her prey, already calm. She didn't feed; the cats were designed to want to kill, but also to dislike the taste of humans. Romi avoided the cleaner-bots waiting with their usual metal patience and requested the cat to come quietly over to him and submit to leash and law.

She came, the look in her eyes more tired than triumphant.

The cat—named Miara—walked slowly, as if weights kept her soft paws down and held her head below her shoulders. Stars and space docks winked in the clear sky above them, the lights of ships coming and going between the surface and various destinations in the Five Worlds. Maybe some were on their way to the Making War or carrying goods or soldiers or parts to supply the fleet from Silver's Home.

Romi found Harrah pacing in the keeping pens, waiting for them. She was tall and thin, with bright red hair caught back in a ponytail and pointed ears as if her mother had been designing an elf.

As they approached, Harrah knelt on the ground, stopping the huge animal's forward progress. She looked into the cat's eyes, her gaze so probing it seemed she searched for Miara's soul.

Romi tried to speak softly and control his voice. "A new weapon. Something that came from the man's fingers."

Harrah grunted. "Where?"

"In her chest and neck. Something too small to see." Romi handed the end of the electronic leash to Harrah and rummaged through the cabinets on the far side of the smooth-floored cave. He returned, handing a visiprobe to Harrah.

She took one look at his shaking hand and snapped. "Calm. Keeper's calm."

"It was a cheat!"

Harrah took the instrument and began to run her hand over the cat's fur, her touch light as a feather, the visiprobe both a slender device cupped in her palm and a screen that splayed out over the back of her hand. "It was an innovation."

"Do you want me to play the last part for you? I think we got the weapon on at least two cameras if I can enhance it."

Harrah shook her head. "Analyze some blood."

"You never watch."

"You will stop watching someday."

Romi grunted. Someone had to root for the animals. He pulled an auto-slide out and pricked Miara's ear in a vein designed to allow easy delivery of blood.

"There." Harrah tilted her hand toward him so the slender screen was easy to see. "If these aren't illegal then the Hunter had the right. The Judge of the Hunt will probably call this for him."

And then more Hunters would use the things. But no Keeper could argue with the Judge. Romi bit back words to that effect and bent to the screen. The slender needles were deeper into the cat's tissue than he expected. Not barbs, like he'd thought. Straight and small. "So, they weren't toxic," he whispered. "But they slowed her down so much I was afraid she'd lose."

Harrah whistled. "Bastard knew enough about engineered paw-cats to slow Miara down by hitting the right nerves."

"Can you get them out?"

Harrah nodded as she stood up and held her hand out for the auto-slide.

"Can we argue that it was a cheat?"

"Unlikely, since he lost." Harrah's voice sounded clipped, disapproving. "It doesn't matter anyway."

Romi didn't know if it was him or the Hunter's trick that made her angry. "Will she be all right?"

"Yes. As soon as these are out they'll stop affecting her."

Knowing Miara would recover only lifted a bit the anger from him.

Harrah reached toward the cat's chest. "Keep her calm."

Romi scratched Miara behind the ears, causing the cat to let out a low rumble. Romi let his arm fall to slide his fingers along Miara's underbelly as Harrah returned with a thin grab-arm and started in on the removal.

The cat tensed under Romi's hand. "Her haunch isn't quite right either. I saw a tremble."

Harrah grunted. Miara scratched at the floor, responding to Harrah's work.

"Someone should have stopped that Hunter." Romi focused on the feel of the thick, glossy fur between his fingers, whispering soft nothings to the cat so her large ears twitched. He liked being companionably close to something so deadly.

"Cheating, even if it is legal." Harrah glanced over at Romi. "Did this one want to live or die?"

"Couldn't tell, except in the end. Then, he wanted to live."

"They all do."

"So do the predators," he protested.

"Yes, yes, I know. They have no choice, while the Hunters do."

He thought about the great fleets massing in space. "Will things will be different after the war?"

"We're Keepers. We protect the humans as much as the beasts."

He didn't like it when she snapped at him. "I know."

"A Keeper's way is balance. If you get too far out of balance some day, you'll lose your place among us. And then what?"

The Keepers wouldn't actually kick him out, but they *could* send him off to some farm with small furry pets for children. "Maybe I'll join the war."

She gave him a long, searching look. "We support the Makers. We are made."

"We're as human as the Hunters."

Harrah sighed. "Everything on Silver's Home is made."

"So then how does it ever end?" Years of watching beasts in his care die might kill him. He kept a tally; up past fifty in four years. The only consolation was that twice as many

Hunters had died. He'd seen one Hunter return three times, until finally a scale-dragon squeezed the life out of him. "We should just let them out. Stop the hunts." He grinned. "But I suppose killing a bunch of innocent people wouldn't be helpful."

"And pay for this place how?"

The argument wasn't new, but surely someday she would start telling him more. She kept secrets. He knew that, they all did. Secrets based on rank, which he would transcend someday. For now, he was somewhat happy to feel irritated. "Are you almost done?"

Harrah nodded, her brows drawn tightly together. "Stay with her a bit, settle her."

"Her haunch needs to heal. It acted up today. I can show you."

"Five days. But keep her in shape."

He never won arguments with Harrah. He should end the session with some grace and say thank you, but when he tried the words wouldn't come.

Romi settled Miara in one of the smaller pens rather than letting her out in the big habitat. He sat close enough to be warmed by the cat's huge body, doing his best to massage the sore spot on Miara's leg. "I'm sorry," he whispered as he worked, over and over. "I'm sorry. I'm sorry."

Far off, he heard the cry of triumph from the Pulla Pens that suggested the vicious little herd animals had won today as well. He was supposed to feel sorry for the lost human, but he couldn't make himself do it anymore. They had become faceless and endless, Hunters with no names and no histories, stripped to the most basic of their enhancements so they fought close to soul and bone. Something else he couldn't understand. When he chose this family, this place, he'd only been fifteen and it had all been magic and mystery and courage. But today's hunt had been sad, the death impossible to understand even if he had cheered for it.

Maybe they were all Made. Maybe the difference between him and Miara was in training. A predator killed. A Keeper stayed calm. Maybe Miara was the lucky one; the cat was doing what came naturally to her.

Romi filed his last report of the day and headed for the Hunting Grounds, the staff bar. A band played soft music in the corner and low conversation filled the room. It smelled of col and alcohol and steaming meat.

He noticed Harrah at a table in the far corner with two other senior Keepers, Kimura and Erick. Probably involved in Senior Keeper talk. He started to turn away but caught Harrah waving him over out of the corner of his eye. He wanted to resist, but it wouldn't do any good. So he went, greeting the other two as he slid into a chair and ordered a Silver Sour.

"Scratch that," Harrah over-rode his order. "Water."

He blinked at her.

"We're here for your promotion test."

"Now?" He thought he had a year to go. Or more. The fatigue—hell no, the despondency—he'd felt earlier shattered into excitement.

"Are you ready?" Kimura asked.

Harrah's eyes bored into his, unblinking.

If she approved his movement up from Junior Keeper to Keeper, he wouldn't have to take orders from her or anyone else anymore. At least not all the time, and not about everything.

Was she hoping he'd fail? Then she could send him away to tend newborns. But that would make her look bad, make her fail, too. He finally quit stumbling over his thoughts and managed to look back at Harrah with true resolve. "I'm ready."

Erick nodded. "What do Keeper's Keep?"

"Safety and balance." Beginner's words, things he'd learned the first day he apprenticed.

Kimura. "Who do Keepers keep safe?"

"Predator and Hunter."

"Why not Predator and Prey?"

"There is no prey on Water Lily."

Harrah asked, "What do Keeper's keep?"

He took a sip of water. He'd already answered this. "Safety and Balance."

"Go deeper."

He pursed his lips. "A place for people who don't have to die to choose an honorable suicide." He meant a place for fools, but that couldn't be what they wanted him to say.

Harrah watched him, unmoving.

"A place for Hunters to prove themselves."

"What do they get for that?" Erick probed.

The first thing that popped into Romi's mind came out. "Sex." He blushed, feeling stupid.

"You're closer than you think."

Successful Hunters did gather a sexual mystique, and some traded on it. But that couldn't be what Erick was probing for. Too obvious, and not something Keeper's influenced anyway. Romi took a slow breath, searched for a different answer. None came.

"Okay, let's approach it from a new angle," Kimura said. "What happened to paw-cats after we got our first genetic samples?"

That was only a few breeding generations ago. "The implants for Keeper's Law, the changes for testing, a lot of immunization, and this version has shorter coats."

"One word," Harrah snapped.

"Evolution."

His mentor smiled. Even though another hour of technical questions followed, Romi felt as if he'd already passed or failed with that answer, and that Harrah's smile had telegraphed *pass*.

When they finished, Harrah looked thoughtful. "We'll tell you tomorrow. Be sure you're ready to commit."

To promise to be part of Water Lily until they didn't need him anymore. It could be the rest of his life.

A Silver Sour didn't sound so good anymore. He stopped to check on Miara on the way back to his bedroom, which was tucked just above the cat pens. The cat raised her head in greeting as Romi settled himself on the floor near enough to trail fingers through her fur, to smell her slightly fetid breath, and gain a swipe of her rough tongue. Miara's power filled the room. He breathed it in, her scent making his nerves tingle with life.

If he passed, he might move on, move to other predators and leave Miara and Harrah.

Maybe that was why the test came now. They wanted him not to care, wanted him to leave Miara and the other cats and go somewhere else to find the balance Harrah was always on him about.

"Evolution," he whispered to Miara. "That's what you're doing. Evolving." Every time one of the predators died, the responsible Makers took the body, the datastream, the tapes, and even its medical records and learned from it all, making future generations stronger. In this way, everything a Hunter tried and succeeded at made the next predators deadlier. It was true, too. He'd seen videos of old hunts. Slow and inelegant. Nothing like the tooth and claw and cleverness of the day, the challenges not so new, nor so clever. Of course, even then predator or Hunter died. But it often took longer now, the hunts lasting whole days or even a few days. In one legendary case, a month.

Keepers had changed too. They had started as an offshoot of the Keepers of Lopali who helped the human fliers, but now they had become their own affinity group inside the greater Water Lily family, separating oversight and care from selling and creating. Business evolution. Water Lily had more power than ever, wielded more influence on the rest of the planet.

This promotion was all he had ever wanted, but it didn't feel good, not the way he'd thought it would. It felt like sour milk and red blood and confusion.

Maybe he should hope they didn't pass him.

Maybe if they did, he should refuse to take the offer. But then what would he do?

He was tempted to curl up next to Miara and cry into her fur. But under Keeper's Law, one never slept with a predator. Ever. Before he left, Romi whispered to the cat, "Keep winning. Win as long as you can."

Miara blinked at him and then started rubbing her face with a paw, the long claws retracted.

The next morning, Harrah met Romi in the common kitchen. She waved him to a seat while she fixed his favorite version of col, a particularly bracing dark brew with a bitter bite that jolted his nerves awake. She took the seat across from him and let him take his first two sips, the coming reveal of the test results a weight between them. There were dark circles under her eyes. Her uniform shirt was the same one she had worn in the bar last night; one white button was darker than the other. Her voice was soft and raspy with exhaustion as she asked him, "Do you commit?"

"So I passed?"

"Do you commit?" she repeated.

"Why did you test me early?"

She sat back and watched him, letting the two questions create a standoff. Silence stretched between them.

An apprentice—a girl with short-cropped green hair and enough enhancement that she had the slow walk of a strong— came in and poured herself a glass of water, giving Harrah and Romi a wide berth. After she left, Romi tried a different tack. "Was it because I care more about the predators? Because I can't keep my neutrality as perfectly balanced as you like?"

"Because we need you. If you don't commit you will never know why."

The word *need* startled him. "All right."

She scowled at him. "Say it correctly."

Here? There would be a ceremony later, but he needed to say it all now, too? He took a deep breath, forcing remembrance. "I commit to the Keeper's Purpose, to balance and fairness, to uphold the law of Water Lily Continent and Water Lily Family, and to honor both man and beast. I commit my life to the Keeper's Balance, the Keeper's Law, and the Keeper's Practice."

"You passed." She stood up and took his cup and hers to the sink. Not like her to wait on him. Or anyone. When she got back she stood over him and said, "Come with me."

"Don't we have to start the exercising?"

"That is no longer your job."

She led him through the Keeper's caverns and across the hunting grounds. Birds called and insects hummed, grounds-bots worked under the guidance of a handful of apprentices. A boring job. He remembered it. Remembered too, how he used to watch the Keepers walk through and how they seemed clothed in silence and mystery and courage. Separate. So he smiled at the apprentices as they passed close. They rewarded him with surprised looks, a flash of gratitude on one face, puzzlement on another.

After they passed into the bigger hunting grounds, Harrah started running. He took off after her. He was faster, newer, younger by fifty years. But she knew the grounds better and she was leading, so he ran at her heels.

They ran silently. The pace drove Romi until it didn't any more, until his body accepted his demands and his mind floated largely free of it. He could almost imagine being hunted. Being one of the predators. Turning, perhaps, to try and make the Hunter prey, which was part of the give-and-take of Water Lily.

Still, he could never imagine the moment of killing a Hunter, nor could he picture himself as a Hunter.

He could be a cat, a snake, a dragon, any being of tooth and muscle and cunning. But wouldn't it be better to be a free dragon? To fly outside of the enclosures and see the mountains and the sea and the floating islands?

They approached the thick wall between the hunting grounds and the Makers' compound. It stood tall and grey now, rather than the usual camouflage of a hunting day.

They passed through a short door in the looming wall.

Harrah led him up two flights of steps and into a building tall enough that its windows showed much of the green island spread across the ocean, its separate enclosures like interlocking leaves.

They entered a comfortable office occupied only by a single woman, a thin blonde with whipcord muscles and a long face. She wore gloves and boots and a single fabric outfit that clung to her body. She felt as wild as the cats.

Harrah nodded at her. "Aliant, this is Romi."

Aliant nodded back. "Well met."

He knew of her. She had worked on the paw-cats, but gained her ascendance as a leading Maker through refining the sense of smell in the dragons, and creating two subspecies with the ability to breed true. Pictures of many of the predators hung on the wall opposite the window, every one poised to strike, all alone, and detailed so that muscle and claw and wing and scale shone as if touched by bright light from just off-screen to the paintings.

He managed to keep his voice firm even thought he was greeting a legend. "Pleased to meet you."

Aliant sat down on a long couch that faced the expansive windows. She gestured for him to sit beside her, and for Harrah to sit beside him. After a few minutes she asked, "When you look down at the island like this, do you see death or life?"

"Death."

"You answered that too fast." Aliant went silent for a long time, looking out over the quiet enclosures and the small pods of people moving around doing the work of cleaning up and preparing for the next day. "This place has been alive a long time."

And a lot of death had happened there. Sure, there was birth and apprenticeship, love, and even long-term bonding. There was the daily work, the easy and hard routines. The happiness of being elite. The knowledge that Water Lily looked out for itself, met unexpected needs. "It still feels to me like it is in the service of death. Every predator dies."

Harrah spoke, startling him with the strength in her voice. "What we do matters very much. The cover of it is death. You saw that. But now you know more. You answered correctly in the test. We are about evolution, and evolution is life. We work to create strength and intelligence beyond that created by nature alone."

Aliant picked up the conversation without a breath between the two women's voices. "What Makers do is about evolution. All of us. Not simply here where it is so obvious I'm surprised when Keepers don't see it."

Romi's cheeks flushed with heat.

Harrah stood up and turned to face him, the light streaming in from the windows turning her dark in his vision, like a halo spilling around her hair but not touching her eyes. "We tested you yesterday because you are ready. We have a job offer for you."

He blinked, swallowed. "A job?"

Harrah continued. "Yesterday, when we were cleaning Miara up after the fight, you mentioned the Making War. Do you know what happens to us if Islas wins?"

"They'll take us over and force the same kind of stupid rules on us that they maintain in their own world."

Aliant leaned back on the couch and took a long breath. "Doubtful. Our intelligence officers on the fleet believe the Silver's Home *could* make a treaty instead. A treaty might force us to give up Making anything with sentience."

Aliant said. "Most of our predators might be considered sentient."

Harrah continued. "If we lose *or* are forced to a treaty, The Port Authority will probably have to close Water Lily. It's morally offensive to Islas."

Water Lily had intelligence officers on the fleet? Apparently, there were more secrets than he had expected. He should be saying something clever, but he didn't know the right response. Probably not that he found it morally offensive as well, if for a different reason. He did not want to stop creating the animals. He just wanted to stop the fighting. He resented every death.

Aliant asked, "And if we win? If Marcus prevails and Silver's Home wins the war, then our rights to anything sentient we do create will disappear."

The very thing that fed them all. And not just Water Lily. Other enclaves, too. No other affinity group specialized in unique ways to die or almost-die.

But they did make warriors, and flyers, and some of the more exotic pets that Family Sonno made were probably sentient as well. Still... "But we could adapt. We could change the predators a little—more claw and less brains."

Aliant answered him. "We wouldn't have the credit. We're sustained partly on long-term fees. And to go backward, to remove the predator's intelligence? That would be wholly un-palatable."

"For credits?" he said, unable to keep the sarcasm out of his voice. Knowing it was dangerous to feel it, and even more to show it. Keepers were serene and balanced and this wasn't the moment or the place to display anger .

"Do you really think that?" Aliant looked at Harrah as if disappointed with her for bringing Romi along. "That we do this for riches? Credit funds our dreams. But we do this for love."

Harrah responded by speaking for him, as if he were a child. "No. Romi understands. He is just young, and more passionate than he will be later." She stopped as if waiting for a response but none came from either Aliant or Romi. So she spoke again. "Go on, Aliant, tell him what we can offer him. He won't spill our secrets."

Aliant's gaze was so searching and intimate that Romi felt small and flayed open.

Harrah spoke to him. "You said you wanted to join the war."

"Didn't you just explain about how neither side can win? It's not like we can create a third fleet."

Aliant laughed. "Of course not. But we can get the Port Authority to let us off-world. We'll join their fleet."

"And fight a space war with blood-and-bone predators?"

"It will work once," Aliant said. "Only once. But imagine dragons loose on a ship. Snakes. Cats."

They were crazy. "They'll just space the air or something. They'll die."

Aliant stood in profile to him, the light of the window reflecting on an almost childish excitement. "They'll do a lot of damage first."

Harrah knew more about how he thought. She said, "They're going to die anyway. You know that. This way they can die against an enemy of ours instead of against humans who are too tired to live."

"They'll live on genetically," Aliant added. "We've made bargains that will assure that. We just need ten Keepers to go."

"Why me?"

Aliant whispered a question in answer to his question. "Can you send the predators after members of an opposing army that wants to live as much as you do?"

He swallowed back his first answer and thought about his options. "Yes."

"Then you'll leave in a week. Your things will be moved to new quarters. We'll start training tomorrow. If you speak of this, you will be considered an oath breaker."

Which meant he would be locked up, or more likely killed. At least, when the secret was this big. "When do I report and where?"

Aliant told him. Then she said, "Good luck. This is important, and we are trusting you and the others going with you. Document what you do, what happens. Prove to the Port Authority that we're earning our berths."

Her tone was a dismissal.

Harrah escorted him back to the door they'd come in through, and when it clicked shut he felt sure he'd never be let back in. He might not even see Harrah again. He sent her a thank-you message, and started the long lope back across the open hunting fields.

As he ran, the glamour of meeting Aliant faded as the idea of space and war and taking the predators sank into him.

He hated it. He hated it more than he hated his current life. Flying so far with so many charges, and all of them bound to die. If it were for some noble cause he could be okay with that, but it was only so they could keep killing and evolving here forever. It was so the affinity group didn't have to evolve into something better.

Aliant was a Maker. She made change.

Harrah had helped him put himself in this box. She wouldn't do this unless there was no other choice.

He trusted them both and didn't all at once.

Despair dragged at his legs, slowing him.

When he arrived back at the caves he headed directly for the cattery.

Miara paced. She stopped as Romi walked up to the large pane, then resumed again. She could manage twenty steps each way, and maybe the same across. Not much room, but that was enough if she was supposed to be resting her haunch.

Romi stood just outside the habitat and watched.

There were hundreds of predators. It would be too much to expect *this* cat to be allowed to go with him. She was already slightly injured and had survived enough fights to be old for her kind. By the time they met the fleet she could be even older. It might take a year.

Romi was not likely to return. He didn't doubt the danger in the assignment. But his job now had that as well.

He watched Miara's powerful muscles bunch and release as she walked, her head turning as if she searched for another cat, another hunt, maybe another victim.

"I'm going to have to leave you," he told her. "Someone else will come."

The cat looked over at him, a small brightness of curiosity rising and falling in her eyes.

"I'm going away to kill a bunch of animals like you."

Miara's gaze showed no understanding.

At least he would be with his beloved beasts. He would remain a Keeper. Of sorts. No part of him expected to bring any of them back alive.

"Miara?" Romi said, then repeated, "Miara," until she stopped pacing and stood, staring at him standing within striking distance.

"I can't release you here," he told the cat. "The Law is absolute inside the caves. But if I could fight you, I would. I would die today rather than leave on this mission."

For the first time, Romi understood the feeling that sent Hunters here. Not enough to get on the waiting list himself, but enough to understand why it existed.

Lament for a Wife

Brenda Cooper

Our parents crossed a void for death,
filled a ship with food and tools
sufficient to fuel a losing fight

Did they know about the stillness
of a toddler taken by a yellowsnake?
How you gave the last smile ever
on your lips to her, and that mourning
takes forever? That your red hair
would be one shade darker
than the flames of your funeral pyre?
Did they feel the warmth of your pale
cheek the last my lips touched you?

What must their life have been
for this to be better?

Found in the notes Paloma made aboard the New Making.

A Note on the Universe

The Universe is always bigger than one story or even one book. My good friend John Pitts wrote a touching, brave story about what might have happened to other people in the greater universe of these stories. I decided to make that that last story in this book for two reasons. It's a great story, and thus a nice note to end on. It's an expansion, and as a writer I want to leave readers with a sense of the larger universe of this story.

MAGGIE

JOHN A. PITTS

Maggie walked out onto the front porch of the cabin, enjoying the bracing cold that quashed the last vestiges of fall. She glanced across the wide expanse of her homestead as the dust kicked up by her soon-to-be visitors spiraled upward into the cerulean sky. She finished the last swallow of her now tepid tea and set the cup on the porch rail, twisting it back and forth on the weathered wood, dancing it around the deep-set ring stain where Aariv had habitually set down his own mug every morning as he watched the sunrise over the hills—back before he'd broken his promise to her and died. The pain of his passing had become a familiar companion these last seven years, a bitter-sweet reminder of the love they'd shared.

She took a deep, cleansing breath, touched her forehead, then her lips, and finally offered her hand, palm up, to the memory of the man who had left her far too soon. After a second breath, she relaxed her shoulders, took up her walking stick, and marched out to meet her visitors.

She walked across the yard to the start of the dirt path that led into town. Here she paused, tugging her shawl closer around her shoulders, and waited. Maybe it would only be her grand-daughter, Kiri. She could hope. Her stomach knotted, warning her otherwise. Maggie set her feet squarely toward the road, folded her hands on the head of her walking stick, and braced for the frustration and rage that would soon roll forth from her beloved son, Anil.

There was just no way around it, not when he set his mind to something. The lights in the sky the previous night would have spooked him, giving him an opportunity to rekindle their ongoing argument about her right to live out here, away from town.

The sun hung nearly three hours above the line of hills, meaning he'd waited until full light, which came late this time of year—her once-brave boy afraid to venture out of the village in the dark.

She could see the look of surprise on Anil's face as he topped the ridge with Kiri following close behind, each riding one of the massive six-legged striders. The lizards did not like the cold, and though they had been engineered by the first colonists to survive the varied weather on Adler's Crossing, they were not very practical. Unless, of course, one wanted to make a strong impression of power.

Maggie didn't care for the beasts. She'd always thought them too much trouble, even with their metabolism geared for warmer days. And don't get her started about their incessant farting and braying, and the piles of manure they left wherever they stopped. She preferred her own two legs, thank you very much. But the beasts were loyal, she'd give them that. Truly, to be fair, they were quite pretty—the way the sun glinted off their flowing scales, hard as steel, supple as leather. The colors had always fascinated Kiri as a small child. This planet had beauty, there was no denying that. Beauty and pain.

By Anil's reaction, he must've expected to find her in the cabin. She smiled and shook her head as he straightened in his saddle, attempting to arrive with some modicum of dignity.

"Oh, my boy," she said under her breath as they slowed further on their approach.

Anil studiously avoided looking at her as he dismounted. She could see by the look on his face he'd come prepared to argue. But the fear she saw in his eyes melted a little of the ice forming on her heart. He did love her, this broken child of hers. He blamed her for Aariv's death, foolish boy. Like it was her fault that sweet, stubborn husband of hers had refused to move into town. Then last winter, Anil and Elenda, had been attacked by night runners killing her and shredding his arm. His grief eclipsed even Kiri's own. When had he grown so selfish? And in the end, all his impotent despair had to be directed somewhere.

Why not blame her for all of it, though it was Adler's Crossing that had taken nearly all he'd loved.

Kiri gave a subdued wave, and Maggie nodded. The young woman turned her attention to her father, watching intently as he struggled off his strider. He shifted his weight and over-balanced. For an instant he flailed, reaching out with an arm he no longer had before catching the saddle horn with the one that remained. Kiri jumped off her own strider and moved to her father's side before he could fall. She braced him as he slid his boot out of the complicated stirrup and quickly stepped back as he shrugged her off.

Maggie sighed. So prideful. She blamed herself for filling his head with ideals that were too hard to live up to. She and Aariv had taught him to believe tales so fantastic that they were hard to comprehend. The stories she'd learned at the feet of her grandmother, her Gigi, had thrilled her as a child. When she passed those same stories on to her son, they had taken on different meanings, created ghosts and monsters.

"Hello, Mother," he said as he stomped toward her. He held his head high, looking over her shoulder like he always did when he was angry. He'd been tall enough to do that since his thirteenth birthday.

"Good morning, my son. What brings you out to your crèche so early in the day?"

He winced at the word crèche. It was a ship word, a word used in the old stories, from the time before her grandmother's generation landed here on this planet. Not something he considered proper. He bit back his retort, a familiar look of mingled exasperation and condescension passing over his face before he spoke.

"Don't provoke me this morning, please, Mother."

She cocked her head to the side to look from him to Kiri. The young woman's eyes were puffy, but her mouth was set in that way she got when she was nursing an argument. So, this wasn't her idea. Good.

"Why are you all the way out here?" he asked. "I'd hoped to meet you at your cabin and talk?"

"Our cabin," she said with a smile. "You grew up here, unless you've forgotten."

Just like his daughter, he pursed his mouth, chewing on the words he held back. She watched the muscles in his jaw tense, and finally relax. "You need to move into town. You are far too isolated here." He waved his hand to encompass the entirety of the world away from the town at his back.

Meaning she was too old to live here alone.

"You were raised here and you survived just fine."

"The wilds took my father," he barked.

And your fair Elenda... and your arm. Why have you never once mentioned those losses to me?

"Your father's death was an accident. You know that."

He glared at that, the ghost of Aariv between them—her husband, his father.

"It is a burden on the village to send others all the way out here to check on you."

The greater good had become his latest argument, as hollow and specious as the rest.

"I've never asked for help, as you very well know."

"I don't mind," Kiri spoke up.

Anil half-turned, glaring at his daughter.

And with that glare, Kiri, her dear one, her only grandchild, and heart of her heart, slunk back a step as if he'd struck her.

It was not the *girl's* fault.

"Any who wish to visit here are welcome, even you." She wished she could reach through the layer of pain that separated them. "Kiri comes out of love." The girl nodded fervently, but her father could not see her. "The others come at your behest. That's *your* guilt, not mine."

He glared at her, tensing for the next round. "You told Kiri that you thought the lights we saw in the sky the last two nights are from the old ships." He spit the last word. His mind likely boiled with the terror he had created around her tales of the ships that had brought them here across the stars, the robots, and the unnatural ways of their ancestors. "If this is true," he looked around wildly. "The diseases they could bring, the violence, the war..."

Her Gigi had spoken of fleeing wars and strife. Maggie found the stories thrilling; an excuse to have her own adventures. She had come to regret telling them to her boy.

This was but another salvo in their own ongoing war. "I am not afraid, Anil." She took a step forward, hand out. The bracelet she'd gotten from her Gigi years and years ago sparkled in the sunlight, the multihued band suddenly reminding her of the striders' scales.

He eyed that bracelet and stepped away.

She let her hand drop. "I'm not leaving my home."

Color flushed his face.

"You will not defy me," he said, his voice low and hard. "I am the head of the council."

"And I am your mother, Anil. You have no authority over me."

He stared at her for a moment, something mournful in his eyes, then turned and mounted his strider again, abandoning the fight sooner than she'd expected.

Maggie watched him mount with a mixture of pain and stubbornness in her heart. "I love you, too."

Kiri glanced back as she mounted her own strider, but Anil, straight-backed and so sure of his view of the world that nothing ever breached his walls, refused to acknowledge her last words.

She did love him, her perfect child, so broken. As they rode up the ridge that blocked her view of the town, he half turned. He held the reins in his one good hand. For a moment, she thought he may have tried to wave when the stump of his right arm moved, but he jerked his strider around and disappeared over the ridge.

She watched the peak of that ridge, fuming. He was not a violent man, not physically, but the hurt burned bright in him. Still, she knew her son. He would not come back out the next day, needing time to work up his courage and anger before he would attempt to forcibly remove her from her home. That just meant she had to take matters into her own hands. When the lights appeared again this evening, as she was sure they would, she was going after them.

It was long past nightfall when Maggie finally looked up from her quilting. By her reckoning it was coming up on midnight. She stood, stretching her back and pushed the quilt frame away. She rubbed her gnarled knuckles and glanced at the colorful design she'd been working on. Gabriel down in town was getting married to Sunil and the quilt was meant to be a wedding present. Maggie was proud of her tight, even stitches, despite how her hands had begun to fail her. She glanced through the gloom of the rest of the cabin, her eyes struggling to adjust from the glare of her single work light. Blinking, she took up her walking stick, hobbled over to cabin's only window, and twitched the heavy covering aside. Cold slithered up her arm as she peered out through the frost-limned window, looking upward into the black sky, searching for the lights she had seen the night before.

Even though her eyes hadn't adjusted enough to catch the pinprick twinkle of the stars, she could tell the foreign flashes that scored the heavens were closer, more pronounced than they had been the previous night.

Anil would be apoplectic, but Maggie wasn't going to abandon her trip to follow the lights in the sky. Something was happening above Adler's Crossing, and she meant to discover its secrets. Anil may very well screw up his courage to return come the morning, so she couldn't wait any longer to start what could be her last true adventure. She just wished she could take Kiri with her. That girl needed to spread her wings. Still, Maggie knew in her heart she was more than capable of going on a little hike in the hills she'd known for her entire life. Let them fret, she wasn't a dotard just yet.

Neither was she fool enough to deny her age. She traded her moccasins for thick woolen stockings that came up to her knees and sturdy lined boots. She'd kept on her prairie dress in anticipation of tonight's adventure, it fell well below her knees and the layers would retain her body heat quite nicely. After she took up her travelling pack, and donned a balaclava, scarf, hat, and heavy coat, she sat to gather more strength. She didn't have the stamina she once did. Hours bent over her quilting combined with her cursed insomnia had begun to wear her down. Not that she'd admit it to Anil.

She loved that Kiri came to check up on her. While some of the others came out to get some piece of aging technology fixed, or just to boss her around, none of them ever wanted to hear the old stories of how they came to Adler's Crossing. Kiri, now…that girl had an imagination. She always wanted to hear how they'd been meant to go on to a planet named Fremont but ended up on this gods-forsaken rock on the edge of known space, circling a feeble orange dwarf.

Most of the townies had slipped into believing tales of the old ones steeped in distorted myths and illogical legends. Gods, some called them, those who flew between the stars in bubbles of air. Others claimed that their ancestors had always been on Adler's Crossing and that Maggie was a lunatic. If it weren't for her own great grandmother, her Gigi, Maggie may have believed just like them. She fingered her bracelet, rotating it around her wrist, thinking how thin Gigi's wrists had been the day she'd given the magnificent heirloom to her. Gigi had always told her how brilliant she was, and how brave; maybe that's why she tried so hard with Kiri. The girl was smart, insightful, and good with her hands. She produced the finest needlepoint and had eyes that Maggie envied. She could perform the detail circuit and crystal work that eluded Maggie these days, if only she would step out of her father's shadow and become her own person. It was hard for a young woman of her age to go against the accepted cultural norms, but Maggie had hope for her.

Once she had her breath back, she made sure to turn off the light to save the charge—waste not, want not, her old Gigi had thumped into her—and threw a cloth over the precious plasticine schematics on her small table. Those were her most prized possessions. It saddened her that her people were devolving into farmers and shepherds when their ancestors had ruled the stars. She sighed in frustration and gave the room one last look before turning to face the frigid night.

The door opened silently on well-oiled hinges, the wood pushing back against her braced arm as the cold wind blasted into the cabin, ruffling the fabric scraps she had been working into the quilt. She had to strain, using muscle and leverage to beat the very breath of nature. That's how she liked to think about her life: a battle between herself and Adler's Crossing. Unfortunately, these days she seemed to be losing as often as winning.

Once she was able to pull the door shut, she fell back against the outer wall, letting her heartbeat slow and her breath settle back to an even pace. The biting wind made the latter more difficult than she liked, but she was stubborn.

"Come on, old woman," she said into the wind and planted her walking stick before her. By her twentieth step, near total darkness engulfed her. She didn't as much as glance back; just trudged forward, keeping her destination firmly in her mind. She knew this bit of land so well, she could traverse it with her eyes closed. She did so on occasion to annoy the others. They were such worriers.

Each step brought her closer to her first destination, and a moment to rest and gather her strength. As she had expected, the walk eased the kinks out of her back and her steps grew more certain. The snows may come again on the morning, but for now it had grown too cold for such nonsense. She stumped eastward.

She didn't have far to go, three hundred steps to the sleeping garden where she planned to plant beans in a few months. Her true objective was the old, worn stump where she would normally sit and enjoy the sunrise during the spring and summer months. There she could rest and watch the skies; get her bearings and determine her next option.

The winter sun, once it rose, would cast a milky glow over the world.

Summer would bring the true beauty of Adler's Crossing, if she lived that long. By the position of the two moons, and the way the Widow's Star was hidden over the horizon, she figured the night was nearly spent and the first moments of the new day approached. Not that she would see the sun for another handful of hours. The world rested, quiescent but for herself and the wind. Even the night runners slept in their dens rather than face this bone-cracking cold.

Two hundred and seventy steps onward and she doubled her resolve. Her muscles had warmed nicely, and she reveled in the exertion. Life was work, and she wanted to live to the fullest. She knew she was prideful, living out here on the old homestead. She appreciated the solitude, yearned for it most times, but these dark winter nights did make her miss Aariv's boisterous laughter, and Anil's bright accompaniment.

With a sigh of relief, she made it to the fence that sheltered her garden. Using it for support, she set off northward for eleven steps where she found the old, worn stump waiting to nestle her backside. She sat, leaned against the fence post, and closed her eyes for a moment. When she opened them, she glanced back toward her cabin out of habit. Only the faintest bit of light peeked around the edge of her window, a tiny shard that told her she had not settled the tapestry properly. That would leech cold into the cabin. Not that she would return to fix it now. Instead, she leaned her head back and stared up into the sky. Nothing strange appeared, and no new noises broke the regular rhythm of her night. Even the night runners had learned to avoid her place. Their skins covered the windward side of her house, helping to cut the chill of the winter storms, and to deter the skittish canines from her door. The skies held mystery but she only a fool ignored the world around them.

She dozed, just for a few moments, she was sure, but the sound of far-off explosions woke her. Lights smeared the sky above her, great flashes of greens and yellows that spoke of burning oxygen and atomized ship's hulls. She'd seen the like before. Twice, actually in the seventy-eight years she has been on Taurus Seven—the name the star charts had labeled this planet, before her people had run the blockade and settled here, back when Gigi had been younger than Kiri.

Her Gigi had taught her things that none of the others wanted to learn, stories of the exodus and her people's flight to a promised land, only to be attacked and left for dead while the rest of their caravan of ships sped onward to Fremont. How their sacrifice had let the larger group of ships escape. Gigi's story of how their small contingency of ships had fled to this back-water system while the rest made their escape still gave her chills. No one had heard of Taurus Seven until they found themselves smashing through the robotic enforcers at the system's outer parameter. Their captains had made the hard choice and chose this planet to land their people on. One of their ships, the *Alameda*, had been destroyed running the blockade, but the remaining two survived to reach orbit around this rock. Unfortunately, those wide-eyed pilgrims, while seeking a place of refuge from the corporations and the impurity of the genetically enhanced, had been part of a technologically advanced civilization. They didn't realize how much they'd come to depend on technology in their daily lives. Adler's Crossing didn't have as much as a network, or any modern infrastructure. The first year here more died from starvation than had died when they lost the *Alameda.*

They adapted, learning from the few bots and vids they'd brought along. Eventually, farming put food on the table of the nearly one thousand survivors. Over time they learned new skills: woodworking, smithing, even weaving and sewing. Necessity drove their choices. The first colonists were long-lived, her Gigi only dying in her hundred and forty-second year. Each generation after failed sooner and sooner. Hard work, poor diet, and lack of advanced medical care had left Maggie as the most ancient of her people at seventy-eight years.

Those pieces of technology that they possessed had grown unreliable and harder and harder to repair over the years. Even the bots had stopped moving after a while. The children decorated them for winter solstice, thinking them statues.

Tears blurred Maggie's vision, forming tiny ice crystals on her eyelashes. She covered her face with her gloved hands, allowing her breath to warm her face.

Three more booms rocked the night, the pressure of the third enough to shake the ground, and send her sliding to her knees. She watched as a ball of fire blazed across the sky and, with a teeth-rattling impact, slammed into the rocky foothills beyond the edges of her lands, out in what the townies called "The Wastes". She'd explored those lands with Aariv, learning about the scrub and the trees, the wild things that called it home, and the intense arid beauty of the place.

She leveraged herself up with the stump, then the fence, gaining her feet with only moderate protestations from her knees and shoulders. It would be light in a few hours. She had water and food in her pack, as well as medical supplies and other survival gear.

The horizon flashed twice more as something detonated in the wreckage. Nothing had come down from the sky since before Gigi died. This wasn't something she planned to ignore. She took up her walking stick and headed eastward. The Townies might rouse themselves to follow in her wake, but she had her doubts. Silly children. Most wouldn't go beyond the tilled fields for fear of the lopers with their razor-sharp teeth, and the night runners who hunted in packs. They were just wild things, easily understood and easy enough to avoid if you used your head.

As the sun broke across the horizon Maggie stopped to eat a bit of breadfruit. She'd walked three kilometers, six thousand steps for her these days. She had left her own lands hours ago, but these badlands were not unknown to her. She knew that in another two or three clicks she'd come across one of the bots that had wandered off to die alone. At least that's the tale they'd told each other when they had come across the forlorn thing.

The light from the fires still glowed ahead of her when she was ready to set off again. That was a lot of something burning there. She figured another click and she'd be high enough into the foothills to see the next valley where she estimated the crash had occurred. She was thankful it had missed her valley, and the four villages.

By the time the sun was fully three thumb widths above the eastern horizon, she found the first piece of debris. She examined the scorched and shredded plating, which she knew was not steel. Words from her Gigi came to her, carbon fiber, made up of individual lattices, which were stronger and lighter than anything they could produce these days. She glanced around, noted the positions of the hills and the sun, made a quick calculation in her head and pulled a small pad out of her satchel. The hemp paper was rougher than the plasticine she inherited from her Gigi, but it was what they had the capability to make. She made a few notes, so she could bring others here to recover the carbon fiber remnants. Whether or not they could figure out how to use them was a worry for another day.

At the top of the next hill she looked down into the valley and followed the trail of destruction with her eyes. The tiny bit of salvage she'd found seemed silly to her now that she saw the wreckage strewn across a kilometer or more. The woods along that path burned, smoke rising into the crisp morning.

That was no small ship. She estimated it to be larger than the four villages combined. The thought of how the town leaders would react when they saw proof that others lived beyond the twin moons brought a smile to her face. Nothing like cold, hard facts to dispel illusions.

Near the bottom of the hill she found the first body. She stood trembling. She was no stranger to death, but the accidents she'd seen had never been on this scale. The being had been near enough to human for her to understand the parts she saw. It wore a hard-cased exoskeleton and she could see two legs and what could've been four or more arms. It was hard to tell if that was even one person, or a couple, with the way it was smashed beneath a section of ship larger than her cabin. She had no desire to examine any closer. Whoever that was, *whatever* that was, she had no doubt they were dead. She moved on, thankful for the cold that tamped down the smells of death.

The sheer amount of wreckage began to overwhelm her. So far, she had found three other bodies, but no survivors. At least these each had only four limbs apiece. She walked past plates that burned with no discernible fuel source, and gave those a wide berth. There were radioactives and dangerous compounds that, she knew from Gigi's tales, could kill you with invisible force.

She made her way to the largest surviving piece of the wreckage, curious about what she would discover. Fire prevented her from taking a direct path. As she circled southward for half a click, she came upon something that stopped her. The bot that she and Aariv had discovered more than fifty years ago was trundling along, making its way to the largest block of wreckage, just like she was. Why this surprised her more than the wreck itself was something she'd have to ponder over later. Perhaps it had been such a fixture in her memories, that seeing it in a different context baffled her.

She quickened her pace in an attempt to catch up to the bot, or at least get within hailing distance. If she called out to the machine, would it stop and turn to her? Only one way to find out.

Fifty steps. A hundred. She gained on the bot. Twice it had to circle back as debris or burning trees blocked its path. By the time they'd both closed most of the distance to the largest debris section, she called out. The bot did not stop.

Not to be daunted, she followed the path the bot left in its wake, catching up to the being near a small door in the side of the gargantuan section of wreckage. *What could be inside?* she wondered, dreaming of technology and wonders from beyond her world.

"Hello, citizen," the bot said in a deep and soothing voice. "This portal is coded for human credentials only. Would it be possible for you to try yours?"

Maggie looked at the bot, open-mouthed. It was not a large machine, only coming to her shoulder. The smooth-domed head rested on the main chassis, and the thin legs ended in two tracks. Several arms snaked out of the central body, like metallic ropes, each attempting in some fashion to breach the door. The fact it had turned its head toward her to inquire about her help, while still operating all six of its arms in independent tasks, delighted her.

The bot waited patiently, its arms examining the door seal, the control panel on the left side, as well as the broken array that had once protruded from above the door.

"Credentials?" the bot asked again, indicating Maggie with one snake-like appendage.

She did not feel threatened, rather she stood mesmerized until it prodded her in the shoulder. She took a step back and glanced down, noticing for the first time that Gigi's bracelet glowed a bright blue. She held up her arm. "This?" she asked.

"I see that you are old," the bot said, its voice devoid of any judgment. "Are you incapacitated in any way?"

Maggie shrugged and stepped toward the door. She looked back at the bot, which had stepped aside, and it nodded to her. Maggie waved one arm in front of the panel to the left of the door and a series of loud beeps told her she had succeeded.

The door slid open nearly a hand-width before grinding to a halt.

"It is broken," the bot said. "Please step aside."

Maggie did as she was asked. The bot stepped forward to grasp the door with three arms, bracing itself with the three others. With a great rending shriek, the door slid further open. If she turned sideways, Maggie was sure she could slip through, but the bot, with its round body, could not.

"Take this," the bot said, thrusting a torch into her hand. She aimed it away from herself and touched the button on the end.

Light brighter than the milky day shone forth, allowing her to see inside the compartment. There was another door within.

"This is an airlock," the bot said. "Perhaps you can go inside and see if there is another way to open this door. Otherwise, I will not be able to respond to the distress call that woke me from my sleep."

Woke? That was an interesting way to think about the bot that had been dormant for longer than Maggie had been alive. She had always assumed that it had lost its charge, similar to the lamp she quilted by. That she had to recharge by means of a solar array she had on her roof. It was not very efficient, but it served her needs. Had the arrival of this ship somehow powered the bot?

Once she slipped past the first door, she found the second responded to her bracelet just as the first one had. Unfortunately, as the door slid open black smoke rolled out, sending her staggering back toward fresh air.

"That is not a good sign," the bot said as Maggie bent over, coughing.

Once more the bot grabbed the edge of the door and strained to move it. To Maggie's horror, two of the bot's arms sparked, and were pulled from their housings. The bot rolled back, shaking, then, pushing aside the broken arms, rolled into the airlock and through the second door.

Maggie stared down at the metal limbs, pondering the detail work it would take to reattach them. Her bracelet turned red all of a sudden and pulsed four times as a horrible shrieking sound emanated from the broken doorway. Maggie dug her walking stick into the rocky soil and trundled away from the wreck, expecting something horrible to emerge. Suddenly, she was thrown to the ground as an explosion ripped through the side of the ship far to her left. She found herself on her hands and knees, her ears ringing. Smoking debris rained down around her as she struggled to cover hear head. Had the bot been destroyed?

She screamed as a jagged chunk of ship sliced through her thick coat and into the meat just below her elbow. She managed to roll against a large rock and clasped her wounded arm to her chest. The rain of burning wreckage continued for nearly a minute before the crashing and pinging tapered off.

She sat up, cradling her right arm, blood drenching her dress. She pulled off her scarf and wrapped it tight around the wound, attempting to stop the bleeding with pressure.

As she sat there, her head swimming and her arm throbbing, she was pleased to see the bot come trundling out of the airlock. It carried a small package in its hands, which it presented to her.

"This is an environmental suit. Please don it and come with me. I am not authorized to release the emergency pods, and I am afraid that the survivors may not last much longer. The power source for this section of the ship has become unstable. We must hurry."

"Help an old lady to stand," she said, holding out her left hand.

The bot took her proffered hand and gently helped her up. "You are injured." It was not a question.

"I'll be fine," she said, picking up the package.

The bot helped her unfold the environment suit and showed her how to put it on. Maggie gingerly unwound her scarf, dreading to see the damage to her arm. Wincing, she stripped off her heavy coat as the bot turned its domed head from side to side. Maggie decided it was an indicator of its thinking process.

"You are the descendent of Gigi Starseeker?"

"Yes, how do you know that?"

The bot pointed to her wrist. "That is her biometric identifier. I knew this young engineer. While you are not her, you must be her blood kin, or the bracelet would not recognize you."

Maggie examined the bracelet her great grandmother had given her from her deathbed. "I just thought it was pretty."

Maggie stepped out of her thick dress and lay it on the rock she had curled against, making sure she did not place it in the splatter of her own blood.

"You must remove all of your clothing," the bot said. "With skin contact it will be able to read your vitals, and perhaps even heal your wound. At a minimum it will stop the bleeding."

Maggie stared at the bot for a moment, open mouthed.

"I will turn around if my presence conflicts with your current standards of modesty."

Maggie laughed. "Only one person has seen me naked in forty years, and no one in the last seven. I ain't much to look at, so do what you must."

The cold bit her skin as she placed her undergarments on top of her skirt. She and Aariv had skinny dipped in their day, but she hadn't been naked out of the confines of her cabin since before he died. Her teeth began to chatter fiercely before she managed to step into the bottom of the suit. Once she had her feet firmly planted again, she pulled the main body upward and over her shoulders, while at the same time sliding her arms into the thin sleeves. The cut on her arm leaked crimson, and she swore as the bot helped her pull the material down over the wound. The fit wasn't as tight as she wanted to keep the cut closed.

"This doesn't seem like it will do much," she said, lifting the fabric helmet over the back of her head like a hood.

She gasped as an electrical current ran through the suit. What had once been a baggy, see-through plastic suit now hugged her body, fitting to her form tighter than anything she'd ever worn.

"If you like," the bot said from where it stood facing the ship, "you can pull up a virtual control that will allow you to make certain parts of the suit opaque to preserve your dignity."

She followed its instructions and a virtual panel appeared above her left forearm, over the spot where her bracelet rested tight around her wrist. With a bit of experimentation, she was able to give herself enough cover to satisfy the more modest of her extended family.

"You people had no trouble with nudity, I take it?" she asked, toggling through the screens until she found the environmental controls and set the suit to keep her as warm as if she were bundled in front of her own fire.

"My people?" the bot asked. "I am an artificial being. I am not one of the synthetics who have transferred their consciousness into mechanical form. I was never born, never grown organically. I was created to serve the crew of the *Lassiter* and I am who I am."

Maggie studied her new friend for a moment. There were so many questions, so many things that needed doing, but she remembered the urgency.

"What do I call you, friend bot?"

"Your ancestor called me Edwin when she was a child. By the time we landed here on Taurus Seven—"

"Adler's Crossing," Maggie said, interrupting.

The bot paused. "That seems appropriate. Captain Adler died running the blockade. The *Alameda* and her support ships fought the synthetics, sacrificing themselves so that the rest could land here and have a life free from oppression."

"My Gigi told me that story."

The bot whirred and flashed. "Adler's Crossing is an apt honor for this place."

Maggie smiled. "And what did my Gigi call you when you landed?"

"Bündhu."

"That's beautiful. What does it mean?

She claimed it meant *Lord of the deep water*, but I found no true references in the ship's data cluster.

She smiled. That sounded like her Gigi. "It's nice to meet you, Bündhu." She gave a short curtsy. "Now what is so urgent I had to strip down and put on this fancy suit?"

"We must reenter the ship and rescue those we can."

She nodded. "All that smoke's going to be a problem.

"Not to worry." Bündhu said, showing her how to access the air scrubbers and oxygen converters.

"Now then, if you will follow me."

Bündhu led her past the metal and ceramic shards that littered the ground around them and to the door. Once they entered the ship, Maggie found the suit had many amazing features, such as the ability to augment her vision, allowing her see through the smoke. She was amazed how well the suit filtered the air around her, allowing her to breathe normally despite all the smoke that choked the passageways.

"How long with the suit filter the air?" she asked. She was mastering the communications portion of the suit slower than the environmental, but Bündhu heard her.

"Weeks," he replied. "They are through here."

She followed the bot down a twisted corridor which had handholds allowing for any of the four surfaces to be ladder or hallway. Bündhu led her around sharp corners and exposed wiring, managing to avoid any open flame. Time seemed to stand still as they made their way through that dark place full of flashing lights and groaning metal. Her people had once lived in these halls, thrived in them according to Gigi. She could barely fathom it.

"I need to rest," she said after a while. Her arm throbbed more than ever and she held it against her chest with her good one.

"The suit will also heal that cut on your arm, if you will allow it." Bündhu said as they pushed through a tangle of wiring and entered a space the bot called a *sick bay.*

Surprisingly, the machinery here still operated. Bündhu spoke of system redundancies and hyper-loop couplings until Maggie tuned out the chatter and called up the suit's interface. The graphical display proved simple enough that linking to the ship's system took no time at all. She didn't hesitate. The thought of the advanced healing that Gigi had described had always intrigued her.

The ship injected her through the arm of her suit. There was no pain, but a cold numbness spread from her wrist to her elbow for a full thirty seconds, then faded away. She twiddled with the suit enough to make the arm translucent and she saw that the gash had not only healed, but there was no scar.

So amazing.

"My people would call this magic," she said, breathlessly.

"The nanobots will likely also repair any other damage you have, so don't be surprised if you feel differently after a while."

She nodded and held her arm up, turning it from side to side, astonished.

With her wrist bracelet, she was able to unlock the protocols that allowed Bündhu to remove the three life pods they found. They pulled each of the pods through the ship and out into the cold light of the day, laying them next to the boulder that held her clothing.

They spent the next hour exploring the remaining, viable portions of the ship, Bündhu leading the way when necessary to protect her from harm, and she leading when her bracelet would grant them access to someplace new. She marveled at how much power she had with the bracelet, which now glowed a pearlescent blue.

Just how large had the ship been? And how may had once roamed its gleaming halls? All of her people could've lived just in this portion of the wreckage, and yet they had only found three survivors. The scale of the loss brought tears to her eyes. She and Bündhu walked down long corridors avoiding rooms littered with twisted and broken things. They were searching for any further survivors they could rescue, any salvage worth taking.

After another hour, they found a second working egress and Bündhu opened the larger airlock. Inside they found a hovercraft and a wagon of sorts that they could pull behind the first. Bündhu drove this around the outer perimeter of the wreckage. They stacked the three life pods on the bed of the hovercraft then filled it and the wagon with anything they could manage to bring out of the ship.

They had not recovered even a third of what was within reach when her bracelet began to pulse red once more.

"Bündhu, what does this mean?" she asked, as the bot rolled out of the hold with a large container.

"One moment," Bündhu said. "I'll check."

She watched him rock back and forth as he spoke with the ship. For machines who shared information at quantum speeds, it took Bündhu far too long to turn back to her. She grew worried once more.

"Well?" she asked when she couldn't take the silence any longer.

"As we knew earlier, the fusion reactor in this sector is unstable. The ship has been diverting nanobots there in an attempt to stabilize the cores. Things are not going well. It advises us to evacuate just in case."

Maggie hurried to the hovercraft and climbed up, noticing that her knees didn't twinge even once. Adrenaline, she told herself.

As Bündhu drove the away, Maggie stared back at the enormous wreckage and the possibilities they would lose if the power source failed.

"There is so much there that could help my people," she muttered.

"I will return in a few days to see if the reactor has been stabilized. I may be able to recover more items."

"I'll come with you."

Bündhu stared straight ahead, not dividing his attention as he'd done before. "If it is safe, Gigi's progeny. Only if it is safe."

Maggie didn't argue. They'd discuss the situation when the time came. She wasn't going to let anyone limit her life choices.

She lay back and closed her eyes, letting the exhaustion drag her down into a comfortable numbness. She couldn't believe she'd been gone less than a day—how much her world had changed in such a short amount of time. The possibilities thrilled her. Still, she knew her own people. This would need easing into. Surely, they saw the crash, but would any be brave enough to investigate? Or worse, foolish. She'd have to warn them away.

When she discussed the possibilities, Bündhu suggested that they go into the first town to warn the others, and they in turn, could alert the other three villages.

Maggie laughed. The bots had been dormant far too long. She could just see their reactions to Bündhu as he rolled into town. They were afraid of anything strange. But while some of them could be real bigots, even zealots, they did not deserve death. She felt fairly sure their fear of anything strange or new would keep them huddled near their homes. None of them had surprised her in more than forty years. None but Kiri, of course.

After impressing upon Bündhu the need for discretion, they agreed to take a more circuitous route back to her cabin where they would attempt to revive the three survivors. They'd delay sharing the news with the villages, especially the council of her own village until the next day. Anil would be livid if he knew she'd gone off on her own, much less explored a crashed spaceship. That was a battle she did not relish. Still, she needed to warn them away from the crash until Bündhu could make sure it was safe.

While Bündhu steered them homeward, Maggie climbed in the back to stare down at the life pods. Each was longer than she was tall, and wide enough that even Anil could lay inside it comfortably. Ice had formed on the outer portion of a mirrored casing and she brushed at it with her suited hand. As her bracelet passed over that surface, lights came on, blue like the first time her bracelet glowed, and strange symbols appeared, scrolling across what she realized was a reader screen. She could not make out the words, but recognized many of the characters from the schematics she studied in her cabin.

"Do not wake them," Bündhu admonished her. "Let us get them to a place of safety first."

She climbed back onto the bench seat and pestered him until he showed her how to operate the hovercraft. She was surprised by the strength of the vehicle especially towing the wagon loaded with all they'd salvaged.

"According to the logs I have been able to access," he said as she accelerated around one large boulder and the pods shifted sideways, "of the original twelve crew members on this ship, these are the only survivors."

"Why did they crash?" she asked, a note of anxiety tingeing her voice as they careened through a narrow valley and out into the open plains north and east of her homestead. She slowed the craft, her hands jittery from the adrenaline. Her heart raced as she thought of the three off-worlders who had survived. She whooped, bouncing in her seat and thrilling at the sheer amazement of the moment. They were taking actual people from another world back to her home. How utterly her life had changed in a few short hours. Kiri would empathize. But Anil, oy, he was just as likely to have an aneurysm.

The return trip was much faster and simpler than the brutal trek she had made the night before. What had taken hours was reduced to no more than forty minutes. She felt exhilarated; better than she had in years. Even after such a long and arduous journey, she felt spry.

"And to think our people eschewed all of this," she waved her hand to indicate the craft, wagon, and Bündhu himself.

Bündhu turned to face her. "What do you mean?"

Maggie shrugged. "When the first colonists came here they had nothing more than they could carry with them, plus a few bots like yourself. How long did you operate before going silent?"

"Seven years, four months, three days, eleven minutes, three seconds, and forty-two microseconds. Local time."

"I always wondered where the ship went."

Bündhu turned to her in the way she'd begun to interpret as inquiry. "Ship?"

"We didn't float down here. How did our people get here with no sign of a ship?"

"I had not realized how little you know," Bündhu said. "I beg your forgiveness. The shuttles that brought you here returned to the *Lassiter*. We never knew why they did not return with more supplies. They went silent and we knew we were cut off. But the ship remained in orbit."

"So, the wreckage is the *Lassiter*?"

Bündhu chuckled, an affectation she did not expect from the bot. "This was the *Revolution*; one of three smaller ships. The *Lassiter* was not built for atmospheric landings. It is far larger than the *Revolution*."

Maggie pondered that new knowledge. The ship that lay crumpled in the next valley had been enormous. Just how large was the ship that brought them across the stars?

They rode ahead in silence after that, Maggie's mind a whirlwind. All their lives were about to be upended and she thrilled at the possibilities, but she was no fool. There were those in the villages who would not only oppose such changes, but they were also likely to be hostile to anything too new, too advanced. She needed to tread carefully.

As they reached her homestead, Maggie settled the hovercraft to the ground as smooth as can be. She turned to Bündhu and smirked.

"You did well, Gigi's Maggie."

She ducked her head, pleased with the praise. *I'm giddy*, she thought. *Drunk on joy and exhaustion.* So much had changed in the last few short hours, and here the old farmstead looked exactly the same. It was as if she'd moved a light year into the future and the Adler's Crossing hadn't caught up yet.

She looked toward the cabin and realized, with a shock, that there was a strider tethered outside her cabin. For a split second she thought Anil had arrived unlooked for, and she felt both anger and shame at the thought.

"That beast should be in the barn," Maggie shouted, surprised at the quickness of her anger. "This cold is cruel to them for long periods of time."

Their arrival had been mostly noiseless, the wondrous machine floating over the ground with barely a whisper. But the sound of her shout drew her visitor from the cabin.

"Maggs," her granddaughter called. "There you are, where have you…" she trailed off, looking up to see the hovercraft, the bot, and the gear. She crumpled to the ground, senseless.

Maggie leapt from the hovercraft and ran to the stricken girl. Just yesterday the thought of lifting her granddaughter would have been laughable but now she found she had strength in her like the old days. She was able to lift the young woman in her arms without as much as an increase in heart rate.

"The nanobots are repairing the damage within you," Bündhu had said to her. Just how far did that go?

She carried her granddaughter onto the porch and settled her in a rocking chair.

"Maggs?"

"Hush, now. You fainted."

Kiri reached out and touched the suit that Maggie wore, her eyes as wide as saucers. "What happened to you?"

Maggie stroked her granddaughter's hair, marveling at the way the knots in her knuckles had simply melted away.

"I'll tell you everything," she said, letting the excitement bubble once again.

There was so much to learn, so many questions to answer, but perhaps this would help her people to find their way once again. As she watched the skin around her wrists grow less lined, she thought of Anil and the loss of his arm. Could the nanobots regrow that? Would that be enough to remove some of the bitterness from him?

"Let me show you our visitors."

Kiri squeezed her hand tightly as she followed Maggie out to the hovercraft.

The girl wasn't afraid. That would do for now.

She stared at her granddaughter as Bündhu came around the craft. The girl laughed and Maggie felt hope return. Hope for a new beginning.

If you enjoyed these stories, the rest of the tale can be found in the WordFire Press Author's Preferred Editions of *The Silver Ship and the Sea, Reading the Wind, Wings of Creation,* and (forthcoming) *The Making War.*

http://wordfirepress.com/authors/brenda-cooper/

Acknowledgments

First, I want to than those who helped fund this book via Kickstarter, and then waited patiently for it to be born. It was a far longer wait than we anticipated. Between us, Danielle and I had family emergencies, deaths in both families, health challenges, and a tendency to shoot ourselves in the foot by saying "yes" to many things.

Which brings me to my thanks for Danielle. She helped with the Kickstarter and with creating this book. She's a thorough and persistent editor, and these stories are all better for that. Even more importantly, she also wrote both a story and a poem in my world. I am ever so grateful for that trust and for her hard work and dedication. I'm pretty sure Mike McPhail helped as well, even if he stayed in the background. If nothing else, Mike keeps Dani whole.

John Pitts has been reading in the world of Fremont's Children since before either he or I had published a thing. We're both many novels into our careers now, and I'm always grateful for his long steady friendship. Friends like John can keep you going when you are ready to give up.

Thanks are also due to Kevin J. Anderson and Wordfire Press. Kevin's support for these books has provided a way to reboot the story, to encourage new readers, and for this collection, new writers. I'm very grateful to him for that.

My deepest thanks go to my family, who have always been supportive, no matter what it might cost them.

About the Authors

Brenda Cooper is a writer, a futurist, and a technology professional. She often writes about technology and the environment. Her recent novels include Keepers (Pyr, 2018), Wilders (Pyr, 2017) POST (Espec Books, 2016) and Spear of Light (Pyr, 2016).

Brenda is the winner of the 2007 and 2016 Endeavor Awards for "a distinguished science fiction or fantasy book written by a Pacific Northwest author or authors." Her work has also been nominated for the Phillip K. Dick and Canopus awards.

Brenda lives in Woodinville, Washington with her family and four dogs.

Award-winning author and editor **Danielle Ackley-McPhail** has worked both sides of the publishing industry for longer than she cares to admit. In 2014 she joined forces with husband Mike McPhail and friend Greg Schauer to form her own publishing house, eSpec Books (www.especbooks.com).

Her published works include six novels, *Yesterday's Dreams, Tomorrow's Memories, Today's Promise, The Halfling's Court, The Redcaps' Queen,* and *Baba Ali and the Clockwork Djinn,* written with Day Al-Mohamed. She is also the author of the solo collections *A Legacy of Stars, Consigned to the Sea, Flash in the Can,* and *Transcendence,* the non-fiction writers' guide, *The Literary Handyman,* and is the senior editor of the *Bad-Ass Faeries* anthology series, *Gaslight & Grimm, Dragon's Lure,* and *In an Iron Cage.* Her short stories are included in numerous other anthologies and collections.

She is a member of Broad Universe, a writer's organization focusing on promoting the works of women authors in the speculative genres.

Danielle lives in New Jersey with husband and fellow writer, Mike McPhail and three extremely spoiled cats.

To learn more about her work, visit www.sidhenadaire.com or www.especbooks.

John (J.A.) Pitts resides in the Pacific Northwest where he hunts dragons, trolls, and other beasties amongst the coffee shops and tattoo parlors.

Check out his award winning Sarah Beauhall series from Tor books and Wordfire Press, or his short story collection, Bravado's House of Blues, from Fairwood Press.

FREMONT'S CHILDREN AFFINITY GROUP

Alyksandrei
Andrew Hatchell
Ann Hutchinson
Art Boulton III
Carol Mammano
Carolina Edwards
Cheri Kannarr
Chris Joseph
Christopher Browne
Curtis & Maryrita Steinhour
Cynthia Porter
Danielle Ackley-McPhail
David Cooper
D-Rock
elizabeth
Elizabeth Bourne
Gryffin
Jennifer Brozek
Jeremy Brett

John A. Pitts
Joy Adiletta
Ken Winter
Kerry aka Trouble
Louise Marley
Mark Carter
Mark Lukens
Rhel ná DecVandé
Robby Thrasher
Scott Schaper
Simon Bisson
Stephen Cheng
Sunny and Ben Jackson
SwordFire
Tasha Turner
Timothy Demko, PhD
Trip Space-Parasite
V. Hartman DiSanto
Vespry family